JUNCTION
TALES

JUNCTION
TALES

written by
Glenn McCarty

pictures by
Joe Sutphin

Fireside
Books™

For Danielle,
ab initio itineris, fideles

Contents

PROLOGUE

In the early years, long before I arrived on the scene, the folks who came to call themselves Junctionites were a ragged collection of misfits. They didn't belong anywhere. Matter of fact, they had nothing to call their own but a spot of land, a few bundles of clothes, and their dreams. But they lived, and they loved, and they grew, as the years advanced. By the time I arrived in town in the summer of 1872, you might even say a fragile little community had sprouted. We kept on pushing, though, just like a little plant. And as we grew, we sowed our lives, and we reaped their legacy—our stories.

Now, maybe you know all this already, but I aim to take it

out and show it to you again. There's something about the way stories grow that's hard to see at first. It's like spring blooming out of winter without a lick of effort, or two young folks who find themselves falling in love, when days before they hadn't given it a second thought.

Stories are inevitable. You do the living, and stories will happen. You just have to take the time to pay attention. So it was with us. We grew together and we harvested stories. Generations roll on, as they always do, father to son, mother to daughter, and stories sprout up from the soil of time and love into something real and true. They become the fabric that holds a place together, the beating heart of its people. Folks may look different or come from different places, but if they share their lives, they share their stories. Those stories become the soul of a place.

Well, these are some of our stories, as best as I can set them down for you. Some are rather tall, you might say, perhaps a bit too far-fetched to be believed. But that's the way it goes. A person passes on a tale to another, and the story changes. It grows, sometimes for the better, sometimes not as much. But when it comes down to you, you've got no choice. It exists the way it arrives in your lap. And it's your story now. What will you do with it?

You'll listen, that's one thing. Then you'll tell it to someone else. And they'll become a little part of your story. And on it goes.

So here are some of the stories of our little place in space and time.

Here are the stories of Rattlesnake Junction, Colorado.

Eugene Appleton
Modesto, California
1912

SILVER FEVER

(1856)

When the boom hit, it was easy. Too easy, some said. A man would march out of the hills on Monday, set himself to scouting on Tuesday, stake his claim on Wednesday, and pull chunks of silver ore out of the earth by Friday. He'd repeat the process the next week, and the next, until he got tired of toting the rocks out of the ground, or his haul got too sizable to protect. There was so much ore in the ground, they said, a man would need to be careful where he shone his lantern for fear of blinding himself with the shine.

But out of life's greatest blessings creeps the temptation for life's greatest curses, they say. Been that way since Eden.

On a cloudless Colorado night in the earliest of those boom days, the sky so clear the stars seemed an arm's length away, a man in black rode his palomino out of a stand of ponderosa pines onto the lip of a wide cliff. By day, the horse would have been a striking butter-yellow, with a mane and tail as white as cream and a cross-shaped white patch across its chest. But under the cover of night, it, like the man, was cloaked in shadow. The man dismounted and looped his reins around a tree limb, then moved forward to the edge of the cliff. Behind him spread the backdrop of the Rocky Mountain foothills. Below stretched virgin woods—juniper, cottonwood, and red cedar, where mule deer, bear, and lynx all made their homes.

The man cocked his head and nodded at the musical twinkle of water. There was a creek nearby. This was the place. Days ago, all of this had been just another part of the wild frontier, running its course as it had for thousands of years.

But all of that was about to change.

The man peered deeper into the blackness below. A few pinpoints of orange light were barely visible within the embrace of the forest. As the man watched, two figures moved about in the light. Then, the lights winked out, and all was still.

The man nodded again. It was as he had suspected. This land's time was coming. The people would soon find the riches. And it would test them.

It was time.

The man returned to his horse and mounted. Prodding it into a trot, he wound his way down from the heights to the land below. Horse and rider skirted the edge of the woods, past the spot where the orange light had vanished moments earlier, until they reached a clearing. The sound of water flowed strong and wild from beyond the clearing.

Here, the man stopped and dismounted. He placed a hand on the horse's flank and muttered to it, then removed a few items from his saddlebag and slid them into his pockets. He lit a lantern and moved into the clearing, pausing at the base of a single willow tree in the middle of the path, and set the lantern on the ground beside him. A cave mouth yawned at the far end of the clearing, set into the hills. The man crouched, spread dry tinder around the base of the tree, and pulled a match from his pocket and struck it. The tinder caught easily, and soon, flames licked upward. The air caught the flames, and as if led by some supernatural hand, carried them up the trunk of the willow. There, in the dark moments past midnight, the man watched the flames overtake the trunk of the tree. Finally, as the blaze licked at the lowest branches, the man reached into his saddlebag and pulled out two large water flasks. He opened them and dumped the water onto the trunk. With a hiss and sizzle, the flames were extinguished. Smoke billowed outward for a few moments, and the man beat it away with his hat until it began to dissipate. Then, all was silent.

The man examined the scorched trunk. The mark was striking, but would it serve as the warning he intended to those who sought to dig here? He raised his hand and pressed his palm hard against the scorched trunk, leaving a white handprint against the charred bark. Then, he returned to his horse and mounted again, making the long, slow ride up to his viewpoint on the cliff.

Somewhere in the hills, a lonely coyote raised its voice in a mournful call, perhaps for its mate, or perhaps in a song of warning for the sleeping world. But few heard it.

And the man had already vanished into the night.

"Heave ho there, Jethro. Get a movin'! Day's breaking, and there's silver waiting to be found out there. You sleep any later, we'll lose any hope of striking it today. Come on, now, get up, I say!"

Bartholomew Adler clapped his hands together, hitched his red suspenders over his shoulders, and poked a toe at the body lying prone under a gray, woolen blanket on the ground in front of him. One leg protruded from the blanket, a bright red sock on the end of it. As Bartholomew prodded, the toe wiggled slightly, and the body began to move. A groan came from under the blanket.

"Whassat," he mumbled. "Quit your nagging, woman. I'm up!"

Bartholomew poked again, digging his toe into the ribs of the body under the blanket.

"I said, Polly!—" the voice trailed off. "Oh, right. Bartholomew, you don't need to go jabbing me. I'm up, I'm up!" A mass of rumpled brown hair emerged from under the blanket, topping a round, scowling face. Jethro stretched, then grimaced. "Whoo, chilly, ain't it? Maybe another few minutes?"

His partner, who also happened to be his brother, was a tall, lean man with a face like a hawk, and narrow dark eyes. He scowled at Jethro and raised a tin cup to his lips. He downed one final swallow. "Ain't got time. Sun's a-rising higher every minute, and we've got to have a good day today."

Jethro sat up. "I know, I know."

Bartholomew moved around their campsite, gathering items and stuffing them into a large canvas knapsack. "Matter of fact, we've only got one more dig in us before our money runs out and we've got to pack it all in and head back to Fremont. I know you remember having to sell our horses last week in Golden? It's put-up-or-get-out time, brother."

Jethro glanced up at Bartholomew. "Of course I know all that. Quit bossing me around. We're even in all of this, fifty-fifty, like we agreed. You don't need to act like my boss-man or something." Shaking his head, he shrugged off the blanket and stood, his knees and elbows popping. "Don't suppose …" he muttered. Bartholomew pointed to a pot resting in the coals near the fringes of a small campfire. "Right," he mumbled, trudging over to it.

Jethro poured the contents of the pot into a mug and took a large swig. Instantly, his face twisted in disgust, and he spat out the coffee. "That's it?" he cried. "That's all I get?"

Bartholomew shrugged his shoulders. "You get up early, you get the fresh coffee. Otherwise, you're liable to get some grounds." He hoisted his pack upright and yanked the straps tight. "Pack your things," he said. "Five minutes."

"Why do you always give me orders?" Jethro asked, wiping his mouth with the back of his hand. "I'm the one who found this spot, and I reckon if I went it alone, I'd—"

"If you went it alone, you'd be nothing but a dried corpse for the buzzards to pick clean in a day and a half," Bartholomew spat back. "Face it, Jethro, you can navigate and strategize digging spots better'n anyone I've ever been with, but when it comes to doing the hard work of surviving, you need me to keep you in line. You ain't got the common sense of a brick."

Jethro shook his head, a fleck of coffee ground stuck to his bottom lip. "You ain't got to say all that, Bart. I thought you 'preciated me more than that."

"Oh, I do. But a man's got to know his own strengths and weaknesses. That's all." Jethro nodded, his face still shrunken. "Now pack up."

Jethro wiped his mug clean with a cloth, then went about packing the few items which comprised his gear. In a few minutes, the two men stood before their small fire ring, the rising sun warming the backs of their necks. A gentle breeze played through a stand of ponderosa pine trees ahead.

Nodding to his partner, Jethro stepped around the fire ring, and the two men set off through the trees. "You keep talking about a creek," Jethro said. "Why we going there?"

"Can you get us there?"

" 'Course I can."

"Then trust me, it's the spot. On t'other side's our Judgment Day Claim."

"Judgment Day Claim?" Jethro asked.

"If we strike it rich, it will be the last claim we ever stake," Bartholomew answered. "Can you get us there?"

"Of course I can," Jethro repeated. The stocky man led the way, pausing every few minutes or so to narrow his eyes and peer at some landmark or another, then nod to himself and veer slightly right or left. Soon, the shadow of a rocky outcropping loomed ahead. The two men stopped.

"Is this it?" Bartholomew asked.

Jethro nodded. "The creek cuts through here up ahead."

"Then what?"

"There's probably a cave just beyond these rocks."

A thin smile flickered across Bartholomew's lean face. "Then it's like they said. Come on." He slapped Jethro on the shoulder and brushed past him. In a flash, he had disappeared around the rocks. Jethro stood silent for a moment, then scrambled after his brother. As he did, he nearly crashed headlong into a stationary Bartholomew, who stood staring at something ahead of them on the path.

"What is it?" Jethro asked. Bartholomew's jaw tightened, but he said nothing. Jethro stepped beside his partner and froze at what he saw.

Twenty paces ahead, the path ended at the yawning mouth of a cave. But the way was blocked by a man on horseback standing directly in front of the cave. The man sat astride a yellow palomino, mane and tail as white as cream. He was dressed in black, from jet-black hat to inky cowhide boots. His face was shadowed with a week's worth of black whiskers, and his eyes were cocoa-dark, splitting the air between them like a pinpoint arrow aimed at its target. While they stared, the horse shifted, tail flicking.

Finally, Bartholomew could take it no longer. "You mind moving aside, fella? That's our claim in there."

The man said nothing. The wind kicked up, and the cottonwood limbs around them began to sway vigorously. "I said—"

"This place is perilous. You are not prepared for what you are planning to do." The man's voice was sharp as flint, and both men flinched.

Bartholomew took a step forward. "I don't think you know us at all, fella. We ain't as beat-up as we look. We'll handle ourselves just fine."

The man in black raised his head and pointed at Jethro. "You will find what you seek, but before you do, be warned. The dangers of your endeavor will consume you if you are not careful."

Jethro blinked. "*The dangers of our endeavor?* What's he talking about, Bart?"

"He's talking about mining," Bartholomew said. "Thank you very much for the word of caution, mister, but we know all about soft spots and running out of air and all that. We're prepared."

The man in black said nothing.

"So, step aside," Bartholomew added. He glanced up, unable to look the man in the eye. "Alright?" he repeated, weaker this time.

"You must not dig here," the voice boomed. "Those who grasp too tightly for things that cannot last will find disaster in the end. Leave, or such a disaster will befall you." He stared again, then raised his reins and guided his horse back around the cave entrance and out of sight through the trees.

The two partners watched the dark figure as it left, the seconds ticking by. Finally, Bartholomew turned toward his partner. "Well?" he asked. "You ready?"

But Jethro still stared at the spot left by the man in black. He raised an arm and pointed. "Th ... there—" he stammered. Bartholomew followed his finger and saw a willow tree in the path, a few yards in front of the cave.

"What is it?" Bartholomew asked. But Jethro continued to point. Bartholomew moved toward the tree, then stopped as he reached it. "Well I'll be." The base of the trunk was scorched jet-black, with a single white handprint smudged against it.

"You think he ... he did that?" Jethro said. "For us to see?"

"Nah."

"But, you heard what he said ..."

"About disaster befalling us, or what have you? Poppycock. And who is he, the guardian of the silver mines, or some such hooey? He's probably a miner like us, thinks every last scrap of land out here belongs to him. So he dresses up in the funeral garb and pretends to be some spook to scare fellas." He paused as his words died away. "Yep, that's what it is. Hmph," he added.

"Yeah, sure. That's gotta be it," Jethro agreed. He stared for another long moment at the blackened willow. Then, he hitched up his suspenders and situated his pack between his shoulders. He followed his brother toward the cave mouth. A careful observer would have noticed that every few steps was accompanied by a slight head twitch, as if Jethro was shaking off some unpleasant thought.

The two men entered the cave, their lanterns bathing the ground in twin pools of orange light. The path bent to the right and sloped slowly downward. Their muffled footsteps kicked up loose pebbles, and more than once, a toe caught on a protruding rock and one man stumbled and threw out a hand to steady himself on the cool cave wall. After one such stumble, Bartholomew threw up his hands.

"Well, shoot. There ain't nothing down here!" he cried. But as the words left his lips, he had stumbled forward into a large, open space. "What in—" he began. He raised his lantern, and his jaw dropped.

The two men stood in a large grotto, twenty feet across. Its ceiling towered above them like an ancient church. A dozen or so feet away stood a wide sheet of rock, which hid the room's true depth.

"Aha," Bartholomew whispered, tongue licking his lips. "Now *this* is something." He stepped around the sheet of rock. Jethro followed, and both men shone their lights on the rear wall of the grotto.

The rock in front of them twinkled like the night sky, with shimmering ribbons of silver sprinkled throughout.

Both men gasped.

"Look at 'em," Jethro whispered. "They're as big as …"

"As big as my fist," Bartholomew finished. "Did you know they could be that big?"

Jethro shook his head.

"You know what this means?" Bartholomew asked. "This is it! We found our Judgment Day Claim. We're going to be richer than the queen of England."

Jethro's face lit up. "Richer than Andrew Carnegie."

"Richer than God."

Jethro flinched. Bartholomew scowled at him. "Don't go thinking about that man in black and his crazy warning. I ain't cussing out God, and I don't believe that man was any sort of messenger, so hush up."

Jethro nodded and slung his pack to the ground. He raised

his pickaxe to his shoulder and tapped gingerly at a huge blot of silver in the wall. "Not too hard at first," Bartholomew whispered. The blade hit the wall with a *chink*, and a few loose bits of rock flew out. The two men glanced around, but the ringing echo was the room's only reply. "It'll hold," Bartholomew whispered again.

Jethro smiled and tapped again, harder this time. Bartholomew stood behind him, face bathed in orange light. A cunning grin spread across his face as he watched his partner digging. His mind began to swim in new directions.

After a few minutes of carefully placed cuts, Jethro set down his pickaxe and slid a Bowie knife from his boot. With quick, deft movements, he chiseled at the grooves around the silver. Finally, the piece of silver wobbled and fell from its spot. Instantly, Bartholomew leapt forward and caught the chunk. Jethro turned as Bartholomew held it up between them.

"Look at 'er," Bartholomew whispered. "She's beautiful."

"Sure is," Jethro murmured. "Give 'er to me."

But Bartholomew ignored him. "She's got to be at least a pound."

"A p ... p ... pound? Why that's—"

"Yes, indeed. We could live on this for a year. And look—" Bartholomew raised his lantern and pivoted. The two men gasped again. They had missed it before from the excitement over the first section of wall, but now, the full panorama came clear. The entire grotto was studded with chunks of silver, most as large as the one Bartholomew clutched in his hand, some much larger.

Jethro's eyes widened. "Are we seeing this?" he asked.

"I sure am," Bartholomew answered.

"We've got to get digging. Right now," Jethro said. His fingers twitched excitedly as he wrapped them around the handle of his pickaxe. "We can't wait for someone else to—"

"Now hang on. Quiet down, and let's do this right. You start flailing that thing around like a dish towel, you'll bring this whole room down on top of us. Besides, there's a limit to what two men can carry out by themselves. We already sold our horses, so we're carrying all of this for a spell. Not to mention if we come waltzing into a claim office with sacks upon sacks of silver, we're bound to attract some attention."

"So?"

"So we dig as much as we can now and bury it somewhere secluded. Tomorrow, we'll find ourselves a good mule, load 'er up, and figure out how to haul it out without attracting much attention."

"You've given this a lot of thought, haven't you?" Jethro asked.

"More than you'll know," Bartholomew said, stuffing the chunk of silver into his pants pocket. Jethro's eyes followed it as it disappeared. "I been trudging my way through the badlands of life for far too long. I ain't about to let nothing stand in the way of me and my payday. Nothing." He fixed his partner with a hard stare. "Nothing."

Jethro swallowed. "I'm with you there, partner. I say we get started right away."

And so, the two men both raised pickaxes to shoulders and began to work away at the silver lode before them. Ten minutes passed, then thirty, and—unbeknownst to them, dozens of feet below the ground—day slipped into late afternoon. A small pile of silver chunks began to accumulate at their feet. Finally, Jethro laid his pickaxe down and wiped his forehead with his bandana.

"I think that's a good start," he said, rubbing his shoulder. "It's got to be close to sundown." He bent and pulled a burlap sack from his pack. Instantly, Bartholomew crouched and grabbed several chunks of silver, stuffing them into his own burlap sack. Before Jethro could bat an eye, his partner had deposited their entire cache into his sack.

"I'll take it out to bury it," Bartholomew said. "That alright with you?"

"Well ..." Jethro said.

"I'll take it," Bartholomew repeated. "Makes me feel good having it close by like this."

"Yeah, but—"

"But nothin'," Bartholomew barked.

"I'll come with you," Jethro said.

Bartholomew's eyes narrowed, but he nodded. "Stay close," he muttered.

Dusk was falling as the two men stood beside the willow tree, both trying not to glance at the bone-white handprint against the charred trunk.

"We bury it, then we go back in. *Side by side*," Bartholomew said. He brushed aside the drooping limbs of the willow to reveal a neat space, nearly fully enclosed by the greenery. "This will do," he said. "Dig." Jethro frowned, but dug his axe blade into the earth. When the hole was finished, he stepped back, and Bartholomew dropped the sack of silver in. Jethro spread enough dirt over the sack to cover it.

As Jethro flung the last clod of dirt into the hole, an idea streaked across his mind like a meteor. It wasn't the first brilliant idea he'd ever had, but it was the first in quite awhile. He knew it was brilliant because of the way his pulse started pounding in his chest and his face grew warm. It was the kind of idea that Bartholomew usually had, the kind of idea he would have had more often if he wasn't always taking orders from the pointy-beaked, hard-faced man he'd hitched himself to for the past few months.

Yes, as Jethro stared at the freshly-covered hole, he pictured the gleaming silver and was pricked by the sharp needles of desire. His fingers began to twitch. He wanted to feel the silver in his own palm, cool and shiny. And Bartholomew was the one keeping him from it. In that case …

No, he thought. He'd heard about this sort of thing. His minister back home had warned him against it. "The gold fever will crawl up into you just as quick as a tick," he said. "The trick is to find some way to block yourself from it. Otherwise, it will possess you."

So Bartholomew is blocking me from the fever? Should I be grateful for him?

Instantly, a second voice in his head—honestly, it was hard to tell if they were different—replied.

No. Not grateful. He's the one standing in your way of being rich!

Of course. He chuckled to himself. That was the right voice. He knew where the silver was buried. He would find a way to get separated from his partner, return to this spot under the willow, and—

He sneaked a glance at Bartholomew. Too late. His partner was staring back at him. Jethro froze, eyes shifting.

"You waiting for something, Jethro?"

"Nope, no, I mean … no."

Bartholomew nodded, eyes still narrowed. "Then, let's get back inside and keep digging. Side by side."

"Uh huh," Jethro said absently, then forced himself into a hopefully-plausible yawn. "It's getting mighty late. Why don't we sack out inside the cave for shelter and keep digging in the morning?" He snuck one more glance down at the silver buried below him.

Bartholomew's squint became a scowl. "I don't think that's a good idea, brother. I've got plenty of energy. Let's keep at it."

Jethro frowned. The voices had gone silent for the moment. But as he returned to the cave and hefted his pickaxe, his fingers resumed their feverish twitching. His legs followed. Soon, his entire body felt as though it was itching with the fury of a hundred flea bites. He squeezed his eyes tight, clenched the grip of his pickaxe tighter, and took a few breaths. Behind him, he could hear his brother chipping away at the rock, regular as a ticking clock. The itching, the chipping, the gleam of the silver—it was enough to drive him mad. He opened his eyes and went to work.

Across the cavern, Bartholomew Adler felt none of the same itching or twitching as his brother. His mind was steady and his purpose clear, so he hefted and swung, hefted and swung, as larger and larger pieces of silver grew visible in the wall. Every few minutes, he would pause from his chipping and pry loose another chunk of silver. Into the sack it went. And back to work he would go.

All of this was done, of course, with regular checks on the progress of Jethro behind him. His younger brother seemed to be having trouble maintaining a steady work rate. And he must have run into some kind of mite. The rhythm of his swings was broken regularly by odd shivers and a frantic scratching at a spot between his shoulders. Bartholomew hoped it wouldn't slow them down. But, he did need Jethro to grow tired of digging soon. Only when

Jethro stopped for the night could Bartholomew spring into action. Maybe it was already happening. Then, Bartholomew could—

But he stopped the sentence before he could finish. It did him no good to get ahead of himself. They had brought along nearly a dozen burlap sacks. Fill two more apiece, take them out and bury them, then repeat. At some point, Jethro was bound to give up. He wasn't as strong as his brother.

"What say we carry these out?" Bartholomew called.

His brother laid his pickaxe down with a clank and turned. His face was sweaty and pale. There was no way he could take a full night of this. Even Bartholomew—more fit for physical labor than his brother—felt like his arms were made of lead. "Yeah," Jethro panted. "That'd be a good idea. I … could use a break." He lifted his one partially-filled sack and slung it over his shoulder.

"You can quit for the night," Bartholomew said. "Just sack out in here while I bury our haul."

"No!" Jethro barked, then softened. "I mean—maybe I'll come with you after all."

Bartholomew frowned. The two men retraced their steps out of the cave. Two more sacks joined the first one in the hole.

"Neat and tidy," Bartholomew said with a wink. "Now let's get back in there."

"Hang on," Jethro said. "I've got to refill my water flask."

Bartholomew's eyes narrowed again. "Okay. But come straight back to the cave. No funny business."

"Are you kidding?" Jethro said. "What do you take me for, Bart? You think I'm going to steal all our loot for myself? Ha ha!" He forced the most honest-sounding laugh he could manage.

"Right," Bartholomew muttered. "Of course not."

Jethro raised his water flask. "I'll be back soon."

"Don't be too long. We've got a lot more digging ahead of us."

Jethro nodded and hurried away. By the time he reached the creek, he was at a full-on dash. "Can't leave Bart alone," he repeated to himself. But a break from digging would be nice …

The creek burbled and sang as it danced in blue-white swirls over the rocks. Jethro set down his gear and sank to his knees, burying his face in the water. He tipped his head backward, feeling the cool water run in ribbons down his neck. Then, he lowered his head and drank greedily. Finally, when his belly felt full to bursting, he sank backward, pleasantly numb from the icy water. He lay still for a long moment, then arched his back and stretched. Without warning, the cool fingers of sleep inched their way up his spine. He closed his eyes, yawned deeply, and—

A tickling on his neck pulled him from his reverie. He slapped at it, but the tickling persisted. Hot air floated across his cheeks. His eyes flicked open, and he blinked twice at what he saw.

A yellow dog stood over him, tongue lolling out of its mouth as it panted heavily. In the dusky twilight, it looked as smooth and gold as butterscotch, a peculiar cross-shaped white patch on its chest. As he stared, the dog leaned forward and gave him a wet slurp across the cheek. Jethro flinched and rolled away. The dog moved closer, its coat glistening with water, and shook itself off. Then, it ambled over to the creek and slipped in.

"Well don't that beat all," Jethro said. The dog paddled downstream a few yards, then clambered onto the bank and shook itself again. Then, it padded back to Jethro and sat beside him.

"Friendly fella, aren't ya?" The dog yawned. "Well, I've got to warn you, if you stick with me, you're in for some hard work. We're going back into the mines, you hear? Think you can handle that?"

The dog raised its head, its deep brown eyes peering at him. Jethro sat up and blinked. "Seems like you understood me just then. Don't that beat all? I suppose a man alone out here could start imagining all kinds of crazy things." He shook his head. The dog shifted and raised his paw. Jethro flinched. Had it laid its paw across the burlap sack? He rubbed his eyes. The dog's paw remained on top of the empty sack. It continued to stare at him.

"What the—"

The dog whined. Jethro leaped to his feet. "You're right, fella. I've got to get back. With me snoozing out here, Bartholomew's capable of anything."

He snatched the empty sack and his lantern and jogged back toward the cave. Behind him, the dog whined again and sighed wearily.

Jethro reached the willow tree and paused. The dirt remained undisturbed. Had he misjudged Bart?

There was a rustling in the bushes, and he whirled. Was Bart coming after him now? He was exposed, with no way to defend himself—

The bushes parted, and the yellow dog trotted out, tongue dangling lazily from its mouth.

Jethro sighed. The dog padded over to him, and Jethro patted it on the head. "I guess it's okay if you stick with me. No harm, right?" He patted the dog again and headed back toward the cave. But as he drew closer to the grotto, his legs began to itch again. He could barely keep his legs moving fast enough to keep up with the fierce needling. He reached the grotto, but heard no sound. His muscles tensed. Where was Bartholomew? Was he waiting to ambush him?

Jethro rounded the bend and nearly stumbled over his pickaxe. He sighed in relief. It was right where he'd left it. He stepped into the grotto and saw his brother. Bartholomew had moved a few feet down the wall, and another full sack lay beside him as he chipped away at the wall.

Bartholomew turned and scowled at him. "You were gone long enough. What were you up to?" he asked. "And what's that behind you?"

Jethro turned. The dog trotted up beside him, ears flattened back on its head. It nuzzled its head against Jethro's palm, and he rubbed along the dog's damp jowl. "He came out of the woods," Jethro explained, instantly feeling guilty for the near-nap. But what did he have to feel guilty about? Bartholomew wasn't his boss.

"Well, get to work," Bartholomew said.

Jethro flinched. "You find a place to wait," he said to the dog, then moved to the wall and raised his pickaxe. The dog whined and pawed the ground once. But, as Jethro moved away, it padded quietly out of sight around the sheet of rock.

Again, time slipped away as Jethro dug out silver chunks from the wall. In no time, his burlap sack began to grow full. He glanced over at Bartholomew, who showed no signs of flagging. In the same time as Jethro, he had already filled two more sacks, and was working on a third. They had begun to tap into larger pieces buried deeper inside the wall. Jethro hated to admit it, but he had no chance of waiting for his brother to get tired and quit digging. His only chance for—

There he went again, thinking about making off with the whole claim, every single sackful of silver. This time, it seemed clearer. Why question himself? This was the frontier. Take what you can get, no matter the cost.

A clank interrupted his thoughts. Bartholomew had laid down his pickaxe and was mopping his brow with a bandana. "Dang, I could really use some water about now. You know what I mean?" he said.

Jethro nodded briskly. "That water out there is mighty cool and refreshing."

"Well, since you know where the creek is"—Bartholomew scowled at his brother—"why don't you run up there and fill both our flasks. I'll carry the sacks out and bury them."

Jethro reached for Bartholomew's flask, then froze, noticing the leer across his brother's face. "Actually, why don't you keep digging and I'll bury the sacks on my way to the creek. Load me up. I'll bury 'em, then come back with the water."

Bartholomew slowly drew back the flask. "You know, I don't feel so thirsty all of a sudden. Let's go a little longer, then we'll take out the silver together. Or I'll take it out myself," he muttered.

Jethro frowned. "You sure?"

"I'm sure," Bartholomew growled. He raised his pickaxe, eyes locked on Jethro.

Jethro stared back at Bartholomew. He glanced at the sacks of silver, then at the wall.

Bartholomew glanced at the sacks, then at his section of wall.

And both men began to dig.

From across the grotto, the yellow dog whined and stood. It padded toward the passage and whined again, but the noise was scarcely heard over the sound of the two men slashing at the rock.

After several minutes of frenzied digging, Jethro paused. There had been a sudden tightness in his gut—well, slightly lower, actually—that could only be the natural consequence of a hasty and miscalculated guzzling of a large quantity of water in a short amount of time. He was stretched as tight as a drum.

"Whoa, Nelly," he said to himself. "That's unpleasant." He stretched toward the ceiling, then down to his toes. But no amount of stretching could erase the pressure increasing by the second.

"What's the matter?" He turned to see Bartholomew eyeing him suspiciously.

Jethro gritted his teeth. "Nothing 't all," he said. Did his voice sound strained? It sounded strained. "I feel *fine!*" he practically shouted.

Bartholomew shook his head. "Well, you sound like a kook, that's for sure." He whipped another sack—his fourth—from his pack and laid it on the floor beside him.

Jethro watched his brother return to digging, his eyes watering from the intense pressure in his bladder. This could not last. No human could dig silver with any amount of force under these conditions. But he couldn't leave. The minute he vanished from the cave, his brother would take off. And by the time Jethro returned—he shuddered to think about it.

He felt a tickling of fur against his hand. The dog stood beside him. It nuzzled him forcefully and whined.

"Great," he said. "Don't you try to get me out of here, too."

Bartholomew paused, axe against his shoulder. "I know what

it is!" he said. "When you went to the creek, you got too greedy. You drank enough water for a team of dadgum mustangs, and now, you're all full up. Am I right?"

Jethro's lip curled again, teeth firmly clinched. "Never mind," he muttered.

"Well, go on," Bartholomew said. "Get out there and take care of business. I'll be right here."

"No you won't," Jethro mumbled.

"What's that?"

"Nuh uh. Let's keep digging."

Bartholomew stared at him, then smiled. "Okay," he said. "Have it your way. Keep digging." He lifted his pickaxe.

Jethro glared at Bartholomew and lifted his pickaxe.

And both men began to dig.

The minutes ticked on, but with each swing, Jethro felt his stamina waning. On top of the pressure, the strange itch had returned, along with the visions of the chunks of silver waiting to be stolen. The prickles raced up his legs, now waging battle with the overpowering urge to relieve himself. He swung. He paused. He fidgeted.

Finally, Bartholomew set down his pickaxe. "I can't stand here watching you suffer like this," he growled. "Just go on outside, take care of your dadgum business, then come right back. It'll take five minutes, and I won't have to keep watching you doing your little dance. You're hardly digging anymore."

"No," Jethro said. "I ain't going nowhere. Not with you standing here—" His voice trailed off.

Bartholomew raised an eyebrow. "What were you going to say?"

"Nothing."

"No, finish your sentence. *Not with me standing here* what?"

Jethro took a deep breath—perhaps the last one he could manage under the circumstances—and stepped forward. "Not with you alone with our claim, so you can take it all for yourself. That's what you've been waiting for this whole night, haven't you, Bart? First, you wanted to steal it when I went to the creek. Then, when you saw I couldn't last much longer with digging—*or so you thought*—you figgered you'd just wait me out. Well, I've got news for you, brother. Aside from the imprudent amount of water I drank, I feel as fit as a fiddle. I could dig for hours. *And you're not taking my share.*"

He finished, chest heaving, and gritted his teeth again as he waited for his brother to reply.

Bartholomew began to laugh. It was a long, slow laugh, his face flickering devilishly in the orange light. And as he laughed, he drew a Colt pistol from his pack.

"And I've got news for you too, brother," Bartholomew said, cocking the pistol and pointing it at his brother's chest. "I'm through waiting. You're going to walk out of here, relieve yourself somewhere outside, and keep on walking until you get to Golden, or Denver, or even clear on back to Fremont, Nebraska if you choose. The point is, *you're not getting any of this silver. It's mine!*"

Jethro stared at his brother, hardly recognizable in the false orange light. All physical discomfort was lost for the moment at the maniacal gleam in his brother's eyes, and the silver pistol facing him. Time slowed as the two men faced each other, the seconds ticking away in a vain search for resolution.

A whine split the silence, then a peculiar splattering sound.

"Oh, great. That's just great." Jethro said. In the corner of the grotto, just visible in a patch of light, the dog had apparently done what Jethro had been unwilling to do. A large dark puddle was now spreading down the slight slope toward the two men.

"Ha," Bart said, gun still trained on his brother. "Ironic, ain't it. Looks like he didn't feel like waiting." His jaw clamped shut. "Now get moving." He wiggled the gun barrel toward the passage.

Jethro paused, weighing his options He opened his mouth to reply, then stopped. He eyed his brother warily, taking in the distance, testing his footing.

Then, he lunged.

Bartholomew was taller, rangier, and had a pistol. But Jethro outweighed his older brother by thirty pounds. And he used his weight to knock his brother backward a full two feet. The pistol flew from Bartholomew's hand and skittered across the cavern floor.

Bartholomew settled himself, stood, and braced himself for a second charge. Jethro plowed into him again, this time sending him against the grotto wall where, moments earlier, they'd been fully occupied with digging. Now, the silver was forgotten for the moment in the midst of their mighty tussle. Back and forth they lurched, grasping and lunging. Neither gained much of an advantage, but there was plenty of bone-jarring pounding and plenty of fists connecting with jaws and bellies.

Finally, Jethro slammed into his brother one last time, knocking the tall man sideways onto the grotto floor. Bartholomew groaned, rolled onto his back, and lay still. Jethro crouched, panting for breath. Gritting his teeth, he shoved hard against the far wall of the grotto, aiming for the pistol lying a few feet away from his brother.

"You're not taking the silver from me. It's mine," he growled. And then, he was off. But though he was so tightly focused— or perhaps *because* of his tunnel vision—Jethro didn't notice the dark, slick patch of ground in his path. He took two steps, and then, everything went sideways as he slipped wildly and went down hard. He lay still, the world spinning. "The—the—" he stammered.

A boot appeared directly in his field of vision, large and brown. He looked up to see the barrel of Bartholomew's pistol pointing down at him where he lay, his coat and pants now damp and smelly.

But as he stared up at his brother, wincing against the inevitable end, his brother didn't draw any closer. Instead, Bartholomew's face twisted in horror at something behind Jethro. Eyes bulging, he flinched and dropped the gun.

"You!" he howled. "You're b … b … back!" He seemed to wilt by the second. He glanced down at Jethro, then at the pistol in his hand, and howled again. "Sweet Bertha Williams, what did I almost do?" He staggered backward, the gun slipping from his hand. Jethro watched it all, but made no attempt to claim the pistol. Eyes wide, he took in Bartholomew's transformation with a slack jaw. His brother sank slowly down the wall, an extended index finger pointing up the passage.

In a flash, Jethro rolled over. But Bartholomew was only pointing at the yellow dog. It sat in the passage, a few feet from the scene of its accident. Unlike the two men, it appeared to be as calm as a June afternoon.

"What was it?" Jethro asked. Bartholomew blinked once, lowering his finger. He shook his head and rubbed at his forehead.

"It's the dog," he said. "But I saw *him*."

"Him? You mean—"

"The man in black. From the tree. With the—"

"The golden horse," they said in unison. And with that, they whirled to look again at the dog. But it was gone.

The two men stared at each other.

"You—you sure you saw him? In here? You know that sounds crazy," Jethro asked.

"I know what it sounds like. But I know what I saw,"

Bartholomew snapped. "At least, I think." He paused. "Mebbe I didn't. Hard to say." He staggered away from the wall, extended a hand, and hauled his brother to his feet, shaking his head.

"You pulled a gun on me," Jethro said.

"I know," Bartholomew said. "I got so confused for awhile there. I kept looking at the silver, and at you, and the craziest thoughts kept marching through my head like rows of little red ants. Like if I didn't keep an eye on you—"

"You were going to run off with all of it," Jethro finished. "I got to thinking the same thing."

"Yep," Bartholomew said. "I turned on you, like I swore to Ma I never would. Dang near blew a hole in you, too."

"I'm as guilty as you, Bart," Jethro said, his face hollow in the orange light. The two men stared wordlessly at each other.

"Well, now look at us," Bartholomew said. "I almost got my head mashed in falling against that wall. And you, well, you stink to high heaven."

Jethro lowered his head and sniffed his shirt. "Reckon I do."

"But at least we got the silver," Bartholomew said. "At least—" His voice trailed off, and he glanced around the grotto.

"Let me guess—you're thinking that even though there's a lifetime's worth of silver in this grotto, a part of you never wants to lay eyes on this cursed place again," Jethro said. "I feel the same way."

Bartholomew nodded. "Mebbe I just got spooked by that man. But right now I'm thinking we bury all our silver in the hole. Maybe some other guys find it, maybe they don't. If we take any of this silver with us, we'll pay for it in spades. I truly believe that. What happened here is just a taste of it. We head for Fremont and never look back. How's that sound?"

Jethro nodded, the vision of the man swimming in his mind's eye. *Those who grasp too tightly for things that cannot last will find disaster in the end.* They had come as near to disaster as they could have, that was for sure.

But had there even been a man in black? Reaching back in his mind for the memory of the previous morning was like grasping for a mist. The more he searched, the fainter the memory got. Finally, he shook his head and gave up trying to remember altogether. He certainly wasn't proud of the man he'd become the past night, that was for certain.

"Sounds good," he answered. "But first, I'm going to go relieve myself."

"You go ahead," Bartholomew said, pointing.

"You mean it?" Jethro asked. "You trust me?"

"Yep. 'Sides, you're the one in the extreme hurry," Bartholomew said with a smirk.

Jethro hefted two sacks and dashed from the cave. His brother followed a few moments later, up into the blueing light of a new day. When he reached the tree, he found a rejuvenated-looking Jethro staring at a freshly-widened hole. They added three sacks and stared at the fourth one.

"We should keep one," Bartholomew said. "Ma could use a new cabin, and we could give her a few shoats as well. We don't have to tell anyone where we found it. We'll keep to ourselves on the road back to Fremont."

"Fine with me," Jethro said. "But first—" He reared back and delivered a swift kick to the one remaining sack. "That's what I think of you!" he shouted as his foot swung down. Then—"Ow-wwwooo," he yelped, dancing in pain.

"That wasn't the smartest move," Bartholomew said. "Now get a move on, brother."

Jethro cracked a wry grin. "Woman, quit your nagging," he said. He hefted the sack and balanced it evenly between his shoulders, then trudged up and out of the clearing beside his brother. Neither man turned to look back.

If they had, they would have seen one monstrous chunk of silver lying against the tree trunk where it had tumbled from Jethro's sack.

Jethro glanced up and stretched. "Sky's clearing," he said. "Fine breeze, too. Good day for walking."

"Sure is," Bartholomew said.

The two men clambered up the foothills, picking their way around boulders as they climbed.

"Oh, and one other thing," Bartholomew said, his voice steady over his labored breathing. "Don't you ever call me a coward for this."

"Wouldn't dream of it," Jethro said, glancing up at the broad morning sky. "What the—" Bartholomew had stopped abruptly, nearly causing his brother to plow into him. Jethro stepped forward, eyes wide in anticipation of a black figure looming before them.

But instead, he saw only a single miner, tall and broad-shouldered, making his way through the pass a dozen feet ahead of them. He carried a small pack from which protruded a pick and a length of rope, and he wore a battered brown hat and jacket. But his most striking feature was an immense, bushy beard which flowed down his chest, stretching nearly to his navel.

The man's eyes popped wide. "Well, howdy. Right early to be running into anyone out here."

Bartholomew and Jethro nodded and exchanged glances.

"Looks like you boys had some luck there," the man said. "That's what I'm headed after."

Jethro adjusted the sack over his shoulder. "A fair bit of luck," Bartholomew said tersely.

"Don't you worry. I ain't going to jump ya. Just want to know if you saved any more for the rest of us," the man said. "Or do I have to head down there and find out for myself?"

"Fella," Jethro said. "Whatever you find down there, you're welcome to it. But you dig fair and square. And don't get caught up in any double-dealings, or the man in black will get you. You dig right, and don't stab anyone in the back, y'hear?"

The man laughed. *"The man in black will get you?"* Well, that sure is some strange advice. You two been out in the sun too long?"

"You mark our words," Bartholomew said. "Fair and above-board. That's the only way to make sure he doesn't chase you down. He's ... he's the Guardian of the Rockies, that's what he is."

At this, the man's face grew serious. "You two ain't messing around, are you?" He paused, studying their faces in turn. "Well, fine," he said slowly. "Fine, I'll take your advice. And I'll thank ye kindly for it." He tightened the straps on his pack and stroked his beard thoughtfully as he glanced down the hill. "I reckon I'll go down there and see what I can see." He stretched broadly. "Think once I get to the bottom, I'll find a good place to catch a few winks. These Rockies take a lot out of you." He paused. "Godspeed to you both. You got names pinned to ya?"

"Adler," Bartholomew said. "I'm Bart and this is my brother Jethro. We're headed back to Nebraska as soon as we get a couple of mounts."

"Fine, fine," the man said.

"And yours?" Jethro asked.

"Johnson," the man said. "Jim-Jay Johnson."

"Where you from, Johnson?" Bartholomew asked.

"Well, I ain't really got a home to speak of."

"Best of luck to you down there, Johnson. And remember the man in black," Jethro said. Bartholomew nodded in agreement, and the three men passed each other on the path, leaving the silver mine to rest peacefully.

For the moment, anyway.

A breeze swirled through the willow branches as the gentle burble of the creek was disturbed only slightly by the sound of hooves. A man in black rode a golden palomino out of the woods and took in the single tree before him. The dirt at its base had recently been disturbed, but the lone figure slumbering a dozen feet from its base had yet to see it. But he would, as he would also learn the truth about the rock on which his head rested.

This was it, then. The land's time had come. When the man awoke in a few moments, a new course would be set in motion. More men would come. Their character would be tested, like that of the two men who had just left. But this place would flourish, he could tell. Its foundation would be secure.

With a click of his tongue, the man urged his horse forward and rode out of the clearing.

The bearded man under the tree stirred and stretched. He sat up, glanced around, and his eyes widened at what he saw.

But in an instant, like smoke, or the tune of an ancient song, the rider had vanished into the morning.

CHESTER WILLOUGHBY'S MIRACLE COWS

(1862)

May 7, 1862

Dear Aunt Pauline,

*   Thank you so much for your gracious reply to my inquiry of February 12. As always, I find your responses timely and wise. Who would have thought an oatmeal bath would do wonders for my poison ivy? You have my undying gratitude, as I am itch-free for three days now. Unfortunately, I am writing again with a prickly situation of a more serious nature. After four years on the American frontier, I find myself at a crossroads. All of the*

enthusiasm I once had for the leather trade has all but dried up, and I am, alas, purposeless. The days are long and tiring. What direction should life take me? What career should I choose? As you have helped me countless times before, I once again seek your wisdom in finding a new path.

I await your reply, O Oracle of the Frontier,
— Jobless in Rattlesnake Junction

May 24, 1862

Dear Jobless,

Fear not! Your situation is perfectly normal. Many of us have found ourselves wandering in the metaphorical wilderness like the Israelites of old, but without a guide to show them the way to the promised land. Do not despair. As advice columnist for the Rocky Mountain News, *I consider it my calling to shape and direct the fortunes of all those in need of life guidance. And so, my advice to you is simple: find a new herd. They will provide your purpose. And I am sure you will not have to wait long. Purpose will come to you like a storm of providence. Have you tried looking up at the skies? Often our deliverance arrives right on our doorstep, sooner than we think.*

— Aunt Pauline

"Aha! She did it again!"

Chester Willoughby raised a fist and rapped on the end table beside him, before carefully folding the newspaper and setting it on top of the Bible. He had been waiting three long weeks for Aunt Pauline's reply, but now, as he hauled himself to his feet and began to pace the floor of his narrow living room, he knew his patience had been worth it. Aunt Pauline had not only responded to his letter, but had given him a surge of energy. This was his twelfth letter in the past six months. But this one was different. Unlike his previous queries about pickling beets or wildlife removal, this one had the potential to change his life permanently. And her answer had been worth waiting for. But her words were cryptic. *Find a new herd. A storm of providence.* What did they mean?

Bending his left knee a few times and cursing the weather for inflicting this cursed stiffness on his joints, he headed for the front door. "Rain coming," he said to himself, then froze, the words still on his lips. He mouthed the words again, then returned to the table and snatched up the newspaper, re-reading Aunt Pauline's reply over and over until—

"Aha!" he said. "I've got it!" He hobbled to the door, the stiffness in his troubled knee loosening with each step. Stuffing his wallet into his pocket, he snatched his hat and coat from the peg beside the door and wobbled down the front steps.

"Ramona!" he called. "Ramona, where are you?" There was a rustling from a row of pea plants across the yard, and a woman's head appeared. She raised a gloved hand and wiped at her forehead.

"Here, Chester," she called back. "What's the fuss?"

He bolted to her, scarcely feeling his leg soreness anymore, as his heart drummed like a team of horses. He slid the folded newspaper into the rear of his pants and attempted to steady his nerves. No sense going off half-cocked here. Best keep his plans to himself until he had gone far enough to show Ramona some results. Then he would tell her about it. Too early, and she would ask a million questions. He sighed. Sometimes, "Aunt Pauline's Advice Corner" was the only thing keeping him sane. And for a man whose life work thus far had been divided between horse grooming, hoof-trimming, and crafting leather bridles and reins, sanity was in short supply. He needed a new purpose. And he had just found one. Between Aunt Pauline's talk of a "new herd" and a "storm of providence," he had all the evidence he needed that his luck was about to change. "Going into town," he said, attempting to sound calmer than he felt. "Pick up a few things. Be back for supper."

"You're a man of few words, as always, Chester," Ramona said. "Could you stop off at the Perkins' and see if Hettie has some sugar for me to borrow? I picked enough raspberries this morning to make a nice cobbler."

"Sure will," he said, gliding around the garden. It was a twenty-minute walk from their modest cabin to the center of town. Ordinarily, he would have hitched up Walter and the buggy, but with his knee feeling as fine as ever—despite the messages it was sending him about the weather—he saw no reason to go through the trouble. The sky was as blue as a thistle, and he was in the mood for a walk. Rattlesnake Creek trilled a joyous melody beyond the trees to his right, and Chester was suddenly struck with the urge to whistle. He strolled up River Street, past Jim-Jay Johnson's slender elm spreading its branches across the town green, the morning sun beaming down warmly upon everything in sight. Had such a perfect day existed since the creation of the world?

Chester swung open the door to the lumber yard office. Behind the desk, Charlie Purcell stood engaged in conversation with a clean-shaven man wearing a tan hat cocked back on his head. As the man turned, Chester's heart leapt! William Richman, cattle baron of Rocky Flats! What a stroke of luck! Or maybe not luck. Maybe something more providential.

Chester cleared his throat, fingers drumming on his thigh. Though he always felt comfortable expressing himself in his letters to Aunt Pauline, real face-to-face conversation had always troubled him.

Charlie Purcell broke off mid-sentence. "Help you, sir?" he asked. Richman turned, and the two men stood staring at him.

Instantly, Chester could feel the familiar heat rising in his cheeks. His throat grew dry, and his fingers began twitching ever so slightly. He could turn around and walk out the door right now and leave all of this behind. If it weren't for Aunt

Pauline and her advice. Yes, Aunt Pauline's advice. It had been so clear.

No. No leaving, Chester, he thought. "Why, I believe you can, sir," he said, surprised at how bold his voice sounded. "You as well, Mr. Richman."

Richman blinked. "Have we met?"

"You're Bill Richman, owner of the ranch out near Rocky Flats." The man nodded. "If you take the San Pedro until it intersects the creek, then follow the creek a ways into town, you end up at my back door. I hear you've got sixty-six head of Texas Longhorn, and the herd is growing bigger every day."

Richman nodded again, taking in Chester's faded flannel shirt and dungarees. "You looking for work?"

Chester's eyes widened. "Work? Well, I'm looking for a new line of work, if that's what you mean. But don't worry, I've already found it. This very morning in fact." He chuckled again and cracked his knuckles against his thigh. There was a twinge in his knee, just strong enough to remind him to stay focused on the task at hand. Time was of the essence, though there were no clouds in sight. Yet.

"And I'll need some advice in a minute or two, so hold tight. But first—" he turned to Purcell behind the desk—"I'm looking to build a cattle pen twenty feet square, on my property. And I need you to sell me enough wood to build it, along with a pound or two of nails."

Purcell cocked his head. "A cattle pen, you say? You come into possession of some longhorn steer I don't know about?"

Chester cracked the knuckles on his other hand, then wiped his palms on his shirt. "Soon, gentlemen. Soon, I will do just that." He flinched. Had he said too much?

"You're getting into the cattle business?" Richman asked, folding his arms. "Hadn't heard about any sales or auctions coming up in this part of Colorado."

"Oh, there aren't," Chester said with a smirk. "So, can you get me the wood, Charlie? I'll need it delivered up to my place as soon as you can, out River Street on the low side of the creek, just before the bridge."

"I suppose I can. If you pay up front," Purcell said.

"Certainly," Chester said. "And can you get it out today? Got to get started on this project. Want to get it done before the storm."

The two men glanced out the window, then back at Chester. "Storm?" Purcell asked. "It's as clear as a bell out there."

"For now," Chester said.

"Now, hang on a minute," Richman said. "I don't mean to tell any man his business, but you say you want to build a twenty-foot square pen for cattle, and it's got to be done today before the rain comes. I see no clouds in the sky. Charlie, are you hearing all this?"

"The storm of providence," Chester said.

"Excuse me?"

"*Purpose will come like a storm of providence. That's* what I'm trying to get ahead of."

Richman shook his head. "Well whatever you're up to, I'd say you should have a mighty fine backup plan. This all sounds screwy to me."

"Sorry you feel that way, gents," Chester said. "But I've got a different path to follow."

"Through the weeds, seems to me," Richman said.

Chester slid his wallet from his pocket. "How much do I owe you, Charlie?"

"Well, give me a minute to do the figuring." Purcell turned and disappeared out the back door into the lumber yard. The shop fell silent.

"Now then," Chester said. "Would you mind answering a couple questions I have?"

Richman snorted and eyed the clock over the door. "I suppose it wouldn't hurt."

"Got any tips on branding?"

"Branding?" Richman repeated. "Now that's a pretty advanced question for a newcomer like you to be asking."

"Well?"

"I've always felt branding's the most important thing a new owner can do. You get a new cow, you got to brand it quick. Rustlers and thieves are always on the lookout for unbranded

cattle. Without the brand, you got no way to prove it's yours."
He glanced at the clock on the wall. "Matter of fact, I've got a
dozen cattle that need branding," he added.

"Uh huh." Chester nodded. "And could a blacksmith make a
new brand for you?"

"He can. But Rucker's out of the shop today. I went by to see
about some new shoes for my broncos and the branding for my
cattle. When you—ahem— get your cattle, you'll have to wait
until tomorrow, same as the rest of us."

"Uh huh." Chester nodded again.

Purcell appeared at the back door, rubbing sweat from his
forehead. "Getting right muggy out there. If I didn't know better I'd say a storm—" He paused. Both men swiveled to stare at
Chester, who simply shrugged innocently. Purcell slid a piece of
paper from his pocket and handed it to Chester. "There's your
bill," he said. "I've got my man Joaquin loading up the wagon
now. You can hitch a ride with him back to your place if you
like."

"Thank you." Chester set a stack of bills on the counter.

"Rattlesnake Creek's been pretty high with all the rain this
spring," Purcell continued. "Not sure it can take another hard
storm. She'll jump her banks."

"That so?" Chester asked.

There was a knock on the front door, and a man with dark

eyes and a bandana looped around his neck stuck his head in. "Wagon's loaded, boss."

"Right, then," Chester said. He thrust out his hand, and Purcell shook it briskly.

"Good luck to you, Chester," Purcell said. "Come back and see me if you need more lumber, you hear?"

"Will do, Charlie." Chester nodded and exited the shop. He clambered up onto the wagon seat. Joaquin flicked the reins, and the wagon started off around the green.

Chester smiled. He could hear the rattle of the fresh lumber as the wagon bumped onto River Street toward home. The ground sloped downward, and the lumber shifted behind them. Chester could see his cabin come into view, a glimpse of the creek beyond it.

Ramona dashed out the front door as they rolled into the yard. She was wiping her hands on her apron. "What's all this?" she asked.

"Over there," Chester said to Joaquin, pointing to an open field on the far end of the property. Joaquin tapped the reins again, and the wagon clattered past the house. Ramona met Chester as he clambered down from the wagon.

"Chester, what's going on?" she asked. "Where's my sugar? And the wood! How much did you spend on that?"

"I've got some building to do," he answered.

"Building? But why? Did you get the sugar?"

"The sugar can wait," he said, turning again to Joaquin. "Let's stack it there," he said. The two men began sliding the boards off the wagon, the pile growing by the minute. When they had finished, Chester slid a bank note from his pocket and slipped it into Joaquin's hand. "Much obliged," he said. "I'll take it from here." Joaquin handed over two paper sacks of nails and nodded, then climbed back onto the wagon and drove away.

When the wagon had disappeared over the ridge, Chester turned to his wife and nodded proudly.

"Now are you going to tell me what all this is for?" Ramona asked.

"I'm building a pen," he said.

"A cattle pen?"

He nodded.

"A wife might need a word of explanation about this, not to mention about the cost," she said.

He nodded again. "I counted the cost, my dear. Don't worry." Suddenly, a sharp pain shot through his left knee, nearly doubling him over. He shot a glance at the sky. "Thank you for the reminder," he whispered. "I know there's no time to lose. I'll get started soon."

Ramona looked up. "Should I be concerned about you, Chester?" she asked.

"Not a pinch," he said. "A new herd is coming, right on our doorstep today. That's what she said."

"That's what who said? Chester, why are you talking in confounded riddles today?"

But Chester was done explaining. With a hitch of his pants, he picked up his shovel and took a post from the stack. With newfound urgency, he started to dig. After the first hole was dug, neat and square and three feet deep, he laid the post on the ground beside it, pulled a roll of string from his pocket and unspooled it exactly six feet. Then, he dug a second hole, neat and square and three feet deep and laid a second post beside it. On he went—laying out the string, splitting the soil, neat and square and three feet deep, laying out post after post. As he worked wordlessly, Ramona stared at him. Eventually, she gave up and went back inside.

But Chester worked on. Four holes, five holes, six, all the way to 12. Only when the final hole had been dug did he drop the shovel, chest heaving. He was exhausted. But how could he stop when he felt so full of life? Wiping his forehead with his shirt sleeve, Chester made his way back around the square, sliding the posts into the newly-dug holes and filling the holes with dirt until each post stood straight and true. Then, he moved to the stack of boards and dragged the first long, straight piece of pine to the space between the first two posts. Taking a handful of nails from the paper sack, he dropped them into his pocket. Then, he hoisted his hammer, raised the plank to the first post, and drove the first nail in.

BOOM

As the hammer struck the nail, a clap of thunder shook the yard. Chester flinched and dropped the hammer. Another jolt of pain stabbed his left knee. He grinned broadly. "Right on cue," he said to himself. He picked up the hammer, fishing in his pocket for another nail. Clinching his jaw, he drove another nail in, then a third. Thick thunder clouds rolled in overhead, and the sky darkened. Chester finished the first plank and moved to the second.

From the kitchen window, Ramona's eyes followed her husband as he made his way around the perimeter. Whatever the cause, he was moving with a purpose she hadn't seen in years. An hour passed, but Chester never turned from his labor, pausing only to mop his brow and occasionally hitch up his pants. She nodded and continued to watch.

The throbbing in Chester's knee increased by the minute, but he continued to work. By the time the first raindrops began to splatter against his face, he had completed half the fence rails.

The rain didn't arrive gradually. No sir, it was as if the thick gray clouds had parted, and a waterfall had opened up directly above the determined man hammering a cattle pen together in his yard.

But Chester Willoughby was not deterred. When the water ran in little rivulets down his face into his eyes, he wiped them dry with the back of his sleeve. When his hammer slipped from his grasp into the muddy ground, he picked it up and cleaned it off, then continued hammering.

Suddenly, he looked up to see Ramona standing beside him, a blanket draped over her head and shoulders. She held out his coat. "Take this!" she shouted above the clatter of raindrops. He shook his head. She held out his hat to him, and he stuffed it on, bending the brim to angle the water away from his face. He smiled.

"Thank you, dear. Where would I be without your faith in me?" he asked.

"I hope you know what you're doing," she said, shoving him into his coat.

"It must be done today," he said. "I have to finish today."

She gave him a wry smile, then dashed back up the front steps and into the house. Chester dragged another plank from the stack and took it down the row to the next post. His boots sank into the deepening mud. Pulling them out, he lifted the next plank and drove the nail through it into the post. He could barely see for the torrent from above. But he didn't let it bother him. He knew what this was: a storm of providence, and he, Chester Willoughby, only needed to be faithful to obey. The rest would take care of itself.

The ground below him was a muddy stew and was already finding the low spots, making little streams which ran down the yard toward the road, when Chester drove the last nail into the last plank and stood back to admire his work. But admiration would have to wait until he could see better. Between the thundering downpour and the dimness of the approaching twilight, the new pen was barely visible.

But it was standing. He had done it. Three completed sides and a fourth side with an opening for entering and exiting. That was important, though he didn't exactly know how it would all happen. Wiping the water from his face, Chester trudged across the sloppy yard toward the house.

Ramona threw open the door and dragged him inside.

"You're soaked," she said. "Get in here before you float away with the crops."

Chester shrugged out of his coat and pulled off his shirt, tossing it into a basket. Ramona handed him a towel, and the two stood silently at the front window watching the water in the front yard rise inch by inch. Soon, it had swallowed the first step, and the entire yard was trembling under the hammering weight of the driving rainstorm.

"The creek," Chester murmured. He turned and ducked across the cabin toward the window overlooking the back yard. He shook his head. It was nearly dusk, and the darkened sky made any view of the water impossible.

Ramona flicked the latch and opened the window. Instantly,

they could hear the sound of the rushing water fifty feet away, clear and steady. "That's fast," she whispered. "Do you think it will—"

Chester's hand closed over hers. "I'm ready," he said. "The storm of providence is upon us, and I am prepared."

"Prepared? For what? Chester, you built a pen."

"The pen is for the cattle. And all of us will be safe and dry in the morning. You'll see."

"All of us?"

He placed a finger across her lips and took her hand, leading her away from the window. The rain continued to thunder down on the roof of the little house, minute after minute, hour after hour, long after the sky had gone black and Chester Willoughby and his wife lay side by side under their quilt. Ramona had stayed upright for awhile, listening to the drumming of the rain on the roof, but had finally succumbed to sleep. Now, only Chester lay awake, a smile tracing his lips as the storm rolled on.

Suddenly, Chester's ears perked up. There was a new sound mixed with the frenzy of the drops on the roof and the regular booming of the thunder. Could it be—? He sat up, heart thumping in his chest, waiting to hear it again. Had he imagined it? Was his mind only playing tricks on him? The long seconds passed, every muscle in his body tensed.

Then, he heard it—a sound as lovely as a church choir on Easter Sunday. And Chester Willoughby smiled a wide, contented smile. Slipping his toes deep under the covers, he tugged the quilt up to his chin and closed his eyes.

It was as if Chester Willoughby's mind was watching for daylight, though his eyes were closed. The moment the sun split the birch trees and spilled a shaft of light through the curtains, Chester's eyes snapped open. Instantly, he swung his legs off the bed and stood up. Ramona remained asleep beside him, a beam of sunlight across her arm. Chester tugged on a blue flannel shirt and buttoned it as he moved into the main room. He was just reaching for his boots when a sound from outside caught his ear. He froze, his left hand clutching his boot, halfway to his left foot. Chester stood and stuffed both feet into his boots, stomping them completely in, as he raced for the door.

He flung the door open. The rain had stopped. All was still, except for the steady drizzle of water from the roof of the house. Tree branches lay strewn about the yard, and one large limb lay across a few rows of Ramona's garden. Half the front yard was a pond, and the remainder was a soup of thick mud and would likely not dry for days, if another rain storm didn't pick up where last night's had left off. It was as he had thought as he drifted off to sleep: Rattlesnake Creek had jumped her banks and cut a swath right through his front yard. Was that what she had meant?

Suddenly, Chester's eyes were drawn to movement in the side yard. Near the pen. He thudded down the steps.

There, standing inside the near corner of the newly built— yes, rather ramshackle, but still completely built in only one day!—cattle pen were two red Angus cows. They stood still, one behind the other, eyes fixed on Chester and ears flicking slightly. The one in front turned, and the morning sun caught its flank, reflecting a shimmering shade of deep auburn.

Chester's heart nearly stopped. "You're here," he whispered, almost as if saying it aloud would provide the confirmation he needed. "You came with the flood."

Eyes locked on the two creatures staring back at him, Chester slopped his way across the yard. Soon, he reached the pen and held out a hand cautiously toward the first cow. She raised her head and sniffed his hand. Chester smiled. "Hey, there, girl," he whispered. The cow took a step closer, and then let out a long, low moo. It was the most beautiful thing Chester Willoughby had ever heard. The cow mooed again, then lowered her head and tore out a small clump of grass. Chester smiled, glad he had remembered to build the pen on the grassy crown of the hill.

He clucked his tongue once, holding out his hand toward the second cow. It shuffled forward, and the sun glinted off its brilliant auburn coat. Chester's eyes widened in disbelief.

There was no brand on its flank. He hurried around the pen

to look at its right flank. Again, no brand. Chester ran his hand down its flank, feeling the smooth coat against his fingers.

"And this one is a bull," he whispered. "One of each. It's a miracle," Then, he turned, thrust his hand into the air and pumped his fist wildly.

"Ramona!" he called, "Ramona, come quick. I knew it! They came! They're here! My cows. My miracle cows!"

THE NIGHT THE
MOSQUITOS SANG

(1870)

Everyone's heard the story from Chester about his cattle. Not sure if I believe a lick of it, though. Tasty beef, though."

"Hang it all, Wendell. Ever since you arrived in this town, I've been trying to make you see. Not everything can be explained by logic. I've been out there. I've seen the cows."

Wendell Jenkins adjusted his suspenders. "You got me there, old boy. I haven't been out there to his place yet. Just the same, a flood dropping cows on your doorstep? Herbert, that's foolishness and you know it. Now, I believe I'm all wrapped up with your haircut."

"Hmph." Herbert Watkins stood, adjusted the toothpick

between his teeth, and flopped into a chair along the far wall, next to Charlie Purcell.

It was hot that Saturday morning in early August. Soupy hot. Swampy hot. The kind of hot that makes your teeth sweat. And, fortunately for the occupants of Wendell Jenkins' barber shop, it was the kind of sticky Saturday morning that made for perfect lounge-and-chew-the-fat conditions. Wendell had already given fresh cuts and shaves to Charlie Purcell and Herbert Watkins, but the two men hadn't demonstrated any desire to leave the shop. Which wasn't surprising. They were experts in the art of lounging and fat-chewing.

Elmer Musselman took his place in the cutting chair, and while Wendell set to work snipping and fiddling, the conversation regarding strange occurrences continued.

"That ain't nothing, really. I've got one for you," Elmer said, leaning forward in his chair. "Took place in my own home, a few weeks ago."

"Now sit up straight, Elmer. Unless you want to look like some kind of crooked-hair kook," Wendell said.

Elmer scowled. "Alright, alright. I'm still not convinced you're a proper barber, anyhow. I don't recollect asking your history 'afore I plunked myself down in your chair and let you come at my head with scissors."

"Hey, that's right," Herbert said.

Wendell sighed and slid his scissors into his pocket. "I recall telling you that I've cut the hair of over two hundred men in my time. Never opened a proper barber shop until I arrived here in Rattlesnake Junction, but I'm qualified."

Charlie whistled. "Two hundred men. How'd you do that if you've never had a shop before?"

Wendell slid the scissors from his pocket and worked them open and shut a few times. "Well—" he began.

"Ah, never mind. A barber's a barber. You boys want to hear about the strange thing I saw or not?" Elmer interrupted.

"Fine, fine," Wendell said. "I'll have to tell you some other time, fellas. *And I ain't going to slice off an ear or anything,*" he whispered. "Now sit tall, Elmer."

Elmer complied, eyes lighting up as he unspooled his story. "So one night, I'm home alone, as Sarah has choir practice at church. I decide I'm going to do a good deed and wash my drawers ..."

Charlie snorted. "You just started, and I'm already suspicious. I can't remember you ever getting involved in laundry. Sarah is the only thing standing between you and abject scruffiness of the highest order."

"Shh! He's just getting going," Herbert said, waving a hand.

Elmer scowled at Charlie. "*As I said,* I decided to wash my drawers. So I get out the washtub and the washboard, and set to work. I'm cranking them out, got a whole two pairs done, and it's only taken me thirty minutes. Just then, I look out the window and see there's a mess of thunderhead clouds brewing to the west. So—"

"Wait a minute," Wendell said. "Wasn't it dark out? How could you see thunderhead clouds?"

"Did I say it was dark?"

"You said Sarah was at choir practice," Charlie pointed out.

"Aha. Well, it hadn't gotten full dark yet. It was … a bright sort of night." He paused. "*Anyway,* the clouds tell me a rainstorm is coming on. How am I going to hang my drawers out to dry properly? Well, just as I'm sitting there puzzling, soap bar in my hand, a gust of wind comes through that open window like a freight train—WHOOSH—I look down, and all the clothes I've been cleaning so carefully the past hour get picked up and carried through the air, right out the window like they was sheep in a row.

"Then, wouldn't you know it, the washboard gets picked up, and the last thing I see is that ole' board coming right at my head. It musta conked me right 'atween the eyes, because the next thing I know, Sarah is standing over me, shaking me something fierce, and she's got a whole mess of dirty drawers clutched in her right hand. I sit up, clearing off the cobwebs, and I see the laundry. 'Why, Sarah, how'd they get so dirty?' I ask. You know what she says?"

"What'd she say?" Wendell asked, smirking.

"She says she found all those drawers scattered across our the floor, right next to a bar of soap and the washboard. She said she found me lying under the washtub. And the entire lot of clothes *was still dirty!*"

The other men burst out laughing. Elmer sat forward, shocked at their reaction. "What's so funny about that?"

"Why, Elmer," Charlie began, "you don't think that maybe there's something you're not telling us about all of this. About how you ended up on the floor and the laundry never got washed?"

Elmer's face screwed up in thought. "Not that I can recollect. It was a mighty, magical Rocky Mountain windstorm, one of the fiercest I've ever seen. What else can carry off a man's skivvies and dirty them up like they was never washed?"

"*Like they was never washed.* Is that right?" Wendell asked. Charlie and Herbert snickered.

Elmer paused. "Now hang on a minute, boys. I washed those drawers, just like I said."

"And the washboard knocked you clean unconscious, is that it?" Wendell asked. More snickering.

"You know, a bar of soap can get mighty slippery when it's wet. If I accidentally stepped on that thing—*wheesh*—I'd be liable to go sailing a yard or two before I crashed into something," Charlie said.

"Might even go sailing into the washboard, wind up lying on the floor, head inside the washtub my wife had set out so I could wash my dirty drawers while she was at choir practice," Wendell added. " 'Course, I'd be mighty embarrassed about knocking myself unconscious with the washboard, so I'd have to come up with *some* explanation of how it all happened." He snickered.

"Now, dang blast it, you both got it all wrong!" Elmer insisted. He raised a finger. "It's just one of them unexplainable occurrences which the frontier can dish out. Storms, sickness, and pestilence. It's like a copy of Egypt out here some days."

This sent all three men into a laughing fit. Elmer scowled again. When the laughing had subsided, he glared at them. "Well, it sorta happened that way," he muttered. Suddenly, his face split in a grin. "Thought I'd get you with that one, barber, you bein' new and all."

"I'm new," Wendell said. "But I wasn't born yesterday."

Just then, the door opened, and a tall, lean man with brown hair and a massive, curly beard entered the shop. He wore a bright red shirt and a wide-brimmed brown hat. His dark eyes glittered, and he clapped his hands together genially as he moved through the doorway, where he was instantly greeted by the four men.

"Well, if it ain't Rubicon Springfield! I was wondering if you were going to venture outside today in this heat. It's a wonder you haven't burst into flames with that wool blanket you've got for a beard." Charlie stood and shook Rubicon's hand.

Rubicon made his way to the third chair in the row along the wall, sighing as he settled into it. "It surely is warm, I'll give you that. But Marjorie likes the beard, and I like it when Marjorie likes the way I look. Just a straightforward haircut, when you can squeeze it in."

"That'll be fine," Wendell said, nodding. "I should be finished with Mr. Musselman here in a minute. If he ever lets me cut, in between all his yapping."

"Fine, fine," Elmer said. "Continue." He settled lower in his chair. The steady snip-snip of Wendell's barber shears resumed.

"Wait a second! Kingman Hill!" Elmer pitched forward suddenly, causing Wendell, whose weight had been entirely on his right leg, to pitch forward in turn. As he did, the scissors plunged downward, impaling the arm of the chair with a *thunk* inches from Elmer's left arm. But he scarcely noticed. Fists clenched, he sat taller in his chair. "You're building a cabin up there on Kingman Hill, aren't you? I heard rumors about it in town!"

Rubicon nodded. "That's right. Things have been picking up in the logging business. Seems a good time to find a place of our own."

"Elmer, why are you playing dumb? I told you yesterday about Rubicon's order for lumber," Charlie said. "You know as well as I do he's building up there."

"Well, I reckon I did, didn't I?" Elmer turned toward Rubicon. "But I reckon you ain't heard about the skeeters up there, have you?"

Rubicon frowned. "Mosquitos? Up on Kingman Hill?"

Elmer rose and drifted from his seat. "When night falls, they swarm by the thousands. That's why nobody has ever built up there, even though it's such a prime piece of real estate. They got mosquitos up there so fierce they'll poke a hole clean through a two-by-four piece of lumber. So fierce they'll suck the blood from a grown hog. *So fierce, they'll—*"

"I believe we get the picture, Elmer," Wendell said, making an effort to grasp Elmer by the shoulders and bring him back to the barber chair.

But Elmer was having none of it. He jabbed a long index finger at Rubicon. "And they swarm, Rubicon. *They swarm.* I heard from Matthias Washburn his dog got picked up and carried clean away by a swarm of skeeters last summer."

Herbert sprang from his seat. "It did? But that ain't possible. Is it?"

"Picked up and carried away, like, say, a string of dirty laundry?" Wendell asked.

Elmer frowned. "I ain't fooling about this one. Maybe I exaggerated my previous anecdote for your benefit, but this one's genuine."

"Then how come I've never heard about these skeeters?" Rubicon asked.

"Well, you've never been interested in Kingman Hill before, have you? And now, I'm telling you."

The men glanced at one another, trying to suppress the smiles leaking onto their faces.

Elmer scowled at them. "You can smirk if you like, but I wouldn't build a cabin up on Kingman Hill for all the tea in China." He paused, seeming to come back to himself for the first time in the conversation. "Without proper assistance, that is," he said mysteriously.

No one spoke.

"Proper assistance in solving *the mosquito problem*," he repeated.

Still silence. A chair creaked, and the faint clopping of horses drifted through an open window.

Exasperated, Elmer clapped his hands together. "Well, gosh darn it, isn't any of you interested in hearing what I mean by mosquito assistance?"

Wendell grinned. "I suppose we just figured you were going to tell us."

"Yes, but it's more dramatic if you bust out with something urgent-sounding, desperate. It adds gravitas to the scene."

"Fine, I'll bite," Rubicon said, pausing to give the other men time to process his joke. They snickered. Then, it was his turn to leap from his seat. "*Holy smokes!*" he cried, waving his arms about. "I'd be grateful for some kind of mosquito assistance! What did you have in mind, Elmer?"

Elmer licked his lips. "Now, this may not be widely-known," he began in a hushed voice. "But I happen to be a certified mosquito whisperer." He nodded proudly. "That's right, boys. I learned the craft from my uncle, Cornelius Walker Solomon Musselman. When I was a lad, I discovered that I had the family talent for being able to communicate with mosquitos. To make them do my bidding. Over the years, I've honed this skill into an almost mystical ability to control vast swaths of these pesky insects, on command." He paused, catching his breath after his exuberant speech.

Wendell slid his scissors back into his pocket. "Mystical, you say?" he asked. Elmer nodded.

"They do your bidding, you say?" Charlie asked.

A few snorts slipped from the men's lips, as faces reddened by the second.

"What do you think, Rubicon?" Elmer asked.

"No offense implied, Elmer," Charlie said. "But that seems about the most pointless skill a human being could possess. Being able to talk to mosquitos. What are you going to talk about? Blood types?"

The four men burst into uproarious laughter, their sides shaking, their chairs shaking, even the room itself seeming to quiver. Elmer Musselman sat pouting in his chair as the laughter rang through the small shop. Finally, he stood and strode briskly away from the barber chair. Reaching the door, he whirled on his heels.

"Why, what's the matter, ole boy?" Wendell asked.

"All I aimed to do was offer a piece of assistance to Rubicon in the construction of his new cabin, so he can avoid some misery at the hands of the Kingman Hill Mosquitos—"

"The *hands* of the mosquitos, you say?" Wendell asked, snorting. A fresh round of laughter erupted. Wendell leaned over and grasped the wall for support while Charlie and Rubicon clutched their sides and rocked in their chairs, tears streaming down their faces. Only Herbert wasn't laughing at Elmer's story.

Elmer flung open the door. "I can see I am no longer valued for my assistance. Rubicon, I wish you well in your cabin-building. I will find a way to demonstrate to you gentlemen I am not the royal jester you take me for. The mosquito problem is real, and I will prove it to you."

And with that, Elmer Musselman bolted from the shop. A hush fell over the room, broken by the sound of sniffles from the three men still recovering from their laughing fit. Herbert still sat quietly, eyes narrowed in thought.

"Well now," Wendell said. "That was mighty interesting."

"Indeed," Rubicon said. He stood and gave his beard a few thoughtful strokes.

"He's mighty passionate about all that, isn't he?" Charlie said. "What do you think, Herbert?"

Herbert stared at the spot in the doorway Elmer had recently vacated. "You know ..." he began.

Just then, the door flew open, and Elmer burst into the shop. "Tonight!" he yelped. "I will be leading an expedition to Kingman Hill to find and dispatch the skeeters once and for all. Anyone who wishes to join me should meet at the town green when the moon is over the elm tree." He paused. "That is all." And with that, Elmer stormed out of the shop. Again.

Again, the shop was silent. Wendell slid his scissors into his pocket. "Well, now," he said again.

"Indeed," Rubicon said. "He's trying pretty dang hard to get our attention with this whopper."

"What do you mean, *whopper?*" Herbert asked.

The three men turned to face Herbert.

"I dunno," Herbert said. "You know I'm a believer in the mysterious and unexplained. Who's to say this ain't one of that sort of thing?"

"Like the miracle cows?" Wendell said. "Really?"

"Quite possibly," Herbert said. "I think that ole' boy's up to something, and you owe it to yourself to find out what, Rubicon. Good day, gentlemen. Thanks for the haircut, Wendell." And returning his toothpick to his mouth, he stood, laid three coins on the table, and left.

Silence settled over the shop. Then, Rubicon stood. "He must have forgotten there's no moon tonight," Rubicon said. "That will make our rendezvous mighty tricky."

"You mean—" Charlie said.

Rubicon nodded and stood. "Reckon I'll check Elmer's tale out first-hand."

"Don't tell Herbert," Wendell said.

"Oh, I think he'll be there too," Rubicon said. "You boys are welcome to come along."

"Not me," Charlie said. "That's one too many whoppers I've heard from Elmer."

"You know, that ole' boy skedaddled out of here so fast, he never even paid me," Wendell observed, stroking his whiskers.

"That right?" Charlie asked.

"That's okay," Wendell continued. "He only got half a haircut."

And another fresh round of laughter echoed around the shop as Rubicon Springfield left, emerging onto South Street and the sultry August morning.

The sweltering heat of the day had swirled away like water down a drain, leaving only the filmy residue of damp humidity. Just before midnight, a solitary figure made his way up River Street, the night's sticky moistness wrapped around his shoulders. His wife was fast asleep, but she had approved of the purpose for his trip before she had nodded off. She had stayed awake for longer than usual, a nearly-completed quilting project keeping her awake. But as she had turned in, she mumbled to him, "You be safe up there," before drifting off to sleep.

Now, Rubicon Springfield stood waiting near the elm tree in a thin cotton shirt and the lightest trousers he could find. Despite the temperature, he had covered nearly every inch of exposed skin. Some might say this made him a believer in Elmer Musselman's tale. He wasn't ready to go that far, though. Bugs were bugs, even if they weren't as ferocious as Elmer had described them. A bandana hung loosely around his neck, ready to be hoisted to his eyes should the moment call for it. His face was well-protected, courtesy of the beard.

Rubicon peered across the town green, then up at the black moonless sky, considering how to find his way. Suddenly, there was a noise to his right. There, at the spot where River Street emptied onto the square, a dark figure moved slowly toward him.

"Who's that?" Rubicon hissed. "Show yourself." But as he finished, he could see the figure was limping noticeably on his right leg, his shoulders hunched. "Wendell?"

The figure raised his right arm in a greeting. There was a scratching, then an orange glow illuminated the man's face. "It's me, Rubicon." Wendell said, holding up a lantern.

"Well, howdy, barber. Didn't expect you would be the first one I'd see out here tonight."

"Looks like I've still got the taste for adventure after all. Did you see Elmer or Herbert?"

"That's funny, I haven't. But I got a late start. I figured he'd already left."

"Right," Wendell said. "You ready then?"

Rubicon took the lantern, and the two moved across the green. "Thanks for the light, by the way," he said as they neared the road.

"Don't mention it. How'd you figure you were going to see, anyhow? That's not very thorough planning."

"Hmm, don't reckon I thought of that."

"Come on, Rubicon, that's quite a slip-up for an old Army man," Wendell said. He paused. "You *are* an Army man, aren't you?"

Rubicon stopped. "How'd you know that?"

"Takes one to recognize one," Wendell said slyly. Rubicon's eyes widened. "But don't go spreading that around," Wendell said. "That's just for us old military boys to keep to ourselves."

Rubicon nodded. "Of course."

"Lead the way," Wendell said. Suddenly, there was a rustling sound, and both men stopped. Rubicon narrowed his eyes and glanced at Wendell. He raised an index finger and wagged it in the direction of a cluster of bushes on the edge of the road. Rubicon nodded and raised the lantern. Wendell crouched and picked up a rock, then turned and tossed it into the bushes. There was a thunk, then a cry of alarm.

"What the—hey!"

Both men snickered.

"I reckon you can show yourself, Elmer. You're the one who told us to meet you out here, after all."

A shadowy figure rose from the midst of the bushes, rubbing his forehead. "You can never be too cautious. There's danger afoot after midnight in these parts. But why'd you throw the—hey, is that you, Wendell?" Elmer shoved his way out of the bushes. "So both of you decided to join me after all. *You believe.*"

"Not exactly," Rubicon said. "Don't mistake our presence for belief. We'll go with you up to Kingman Hill. I'm not too sure about the other stuff."

"No way," Elmer said. "You're here. *You believe.*"

"We'll see about that," Wendell said. "Far as I'm concerned, this is a bunch of hooey. But if it means you not getting folks all riled up in my shop with your stories, I'm in favor of proving you wrong."

"Proving me wrong?" Elmer's eyes bulged. "I'm deeply offended." He ambled over to the two men. "I could have sworn Herbert would meet me out here. You fellas seen him tonight?"

Wendell and Rubicon shook their heads.

"No matter," Elmer said. He moved closer. "You got protection?"

"I've got long sleeves and face covering, if that's what you mean. So does he," Rubicon answered.

"Ah," Elmer said, now fully visible in the orange lantern light. "See, you were thinking of protection from ordinary skeeters. But I'm protected from *the other kind*."

"The other kind?" Wendell asked.

"*The Kingman Hill super-skeeters, that's what*," Elmer whispered.

"Ahhh," Rubicon said. "So that's why you've got the stick."

"This *staff*," Elmer began, scowling at Rubicon, "is carved with a variety of sigils used in a secret Arapahoe ceremony to rid the land of pestilence. I cannot speak the words aloud. The symbols are too powerful."

"That one looks like a duck," Wendell observed, pointing.

"It's not a duck," Elmer said. "As I mentioned, these are mystical symbols. When in my possession, the potent powers of this staff will protect all who accompany me."

"Wonderful," Rubicon said dryly. "I was getting worried. But won't you be warm in that shawl?"

"This is no ordinary shawl. It was knitted for me by Rosie Ingersoll herself before she left town under, ahem, mysterious circumstances."

"I didn't think they were mysterious. She stole Cyrus Hathaway's buggy and lit out for Utah. The Marshalls caught her. She was as crooked as a miner's back."

"Be that as it may, this shawl is powerful. Woven into the threads are actual goose feathers because, as we all know, the goose is a natural predator of a mosquito."

"Is that where you got it?" Rubicon said. "Well, your mystical shawl of protection looks in this light to be a lovely shade of lavender. Shall we continue?"

"That's not all, gents," Elmer continued. His fingers wiggled excitedly as he reached for a small satchel slung over his shoulder. "Here we have the *pièce de résistance*," he added, loosening the satchel and pulling out a small glass jar. "*That's British,*" he whispered. Inside the jar was a tan liquid. With trembling hands, Elmer unscrewed the lid and held out the jar. "Inhale."

The two men exchanged glances. "You first," Wendell said. Rubicon leaned closer and breathed in. Instantly, he jerked backward, coughing and waving his hand wildly in front of his face. "That … is … foul," he said. "What's in there? Frog guts?"

Elmer nodded proudly. "You have quite a sniffer there, Rubicon. This one is an Elmer Musselman original. Took me quite a pile of catch-and-squash sessions, but in this jar are the precious innards of two-dozen bullfrogs, preserved for topical application on just such an occasion."

"Topical … application?" Wendell repeated slowly, glancing from Elmer to Rubicon. "You mean, you're going to—"

Elmer's hand plunged into the jar and emerged with a palmful of thick, amber-colored liquid the consistency of maple syrup. As the other two men stared slack-jawed, he rubbed it between his palms and began smearing it up and down his forearms.

"Oh my heavens," Wendell said.

"He's really doing it," Rubicon added.

"Scoff if you will, but I will be protected by the spirit of the American bullfrog, the mortal enemy of mosquitos everywhere. One whiff of this and the super-skeeters will be skedaddling. I have become the predator. *They will fear me.*"

"I see," Wendell said, watching as Elmer scooped out another palmful of liquid and smeared his neck, cheeks, and forehead, then rolled up his pants and applied the goo liberally to his legs.

"Yes, thanks to the staff, the shawl, and my own mosquito repellant, I will be protected body, soul, and spirit, whatever we face. This should provide me enough protection so I can begin communicating with the skeeters without interruption. Then, you will witness something truly remarkable." He paused. "You boys will have to stick with me for safety, or else—" He drew a hand slowly across his throat. "Lead on, Rubicon."

"Right, got it," Rubicon said. "But would you mind staying a few paces behind us? I'm liable to pass out from that frog goop."

"Not too far," Elmer said. "Not too far."

Rubicon raised the lantern, and the three men headed up North Street. But as they moved, Wendell noted the singing of the crickets was growing fainter. It had to be a trick of the ears, or the heat of the night. But it was almost as if a bubble of silence extended outward from their position, moving with them as they walked. Wendell shook his head. There was no way he was linking whatever Elmer Musselman was carrying, or wearing, to the lack of insect noises. That was going too far. But still—

They reached the border of the woods. Rubicon held his lantern at arm's length.

"Would you mind moving over a bit?" Wendell asked Elmer. "I think the wind shifted."

"I ain't moving. It's for your own good, you know," Elmer said.

"I'll be the judge of that," Wendell said. Suddenly, he pointed into the darkness. "Look!"

Rubicon raised the lantern. The three men squinted into the woods. A figure could be seen a hundred or so yards ahead, moving through the trees.

"Who in tarnation is that?" Wendell whispered.

"It's Herbert!" Rubicon hissed back. "I'd recognize that ole' bean pole even without a trace of moonlight. He's probably got Fiddlestick with him, too. You hear his collar jingling?"

"I knew he believed me!" Elmer whispered excitedly. "But why is he up ahead? Didn't he wait for us?"

"No moon," Wendell said.

"Huh?"

"You told us to meet you when the moon is over the elm tree. There's no moon tonight, so he probably just showed up, got tired of waiting, and figured he'd meet you up there."

"But if he's way ahead of us, he won't benefit from my protection," Elmer said. "He's all alone against the elements."

"Poor him," Rubicon said. "He'll just have to do his best. Let's tell him we're here."

"No!" Elmer fairly shrieked. "If we raise our voices, we'll most certainly alert the skeeters to our presence. And if they're alarmed, I won't be able to communicate with them. Even with protection, that's not a fury I wish to call down upon us. We'll have to catch up to him."

"Fine, fine. No skeeter fury. Let's go," Rubicon said. Drawing the lantern tight against his hip, he crept forward. The three men made their way single file into the dark woods, the crunching sound of Herbert Watkins ahead of them faint, but steady. They wove their way through the belly of the forest for half an hour, stopping every few minutes to listen for the sound of man and dog. Each time, their patience was repaid with the familiar echo of snapping twigs and crunching leaves.

"We're heading uphill," Wendell hissed on one such occasion. "We must be getting close."

"I think we're gaining on him," Elmer said.

"I know this ravine," Rubicon said. "It goes up sharply from here. We're almost to Kingman Hill. We've got to clear a path up here once the cabin is built."

Instantly, the three men's pulses began to race. They froze, waiting for the familiar sound of Herbert.

Suddenly, a wild hooting erupted from the trees above them. Then, the sound of a frenzied flapping of wings. Rubicon raised his arms high above his head, the lantern light whipping frantically. An immense shadow plunged over them, whizzed past Wendell's head, and soared off behind them. Wendell staggered backward, hands flailing. As he felt his heartbeat settle, he swallowed hard.

"Owl," he said. "Wasn't that a fright?"

Rubicon steadied the lantern. "Just when you think you're ready for anything …" he said with a chuckle. "You okay, Elmer?"

Elmer leaned idly against a tree, arms folded across his chest. "You see that?" he asked. "That bird didn't even come within ten feet of me. It knew better."

Rubicon shook his head. "Because of your magic shawl, is that right?"

"I thought that only worked on mosquitos, or was it all insects?" Wendell asked.

"Birds, bugs. *Its power is growing.*"

"Hooey," Wendell said. "Let's get going."

"I hope we didn't lose Herbert in all of that confusion," Elmer said. He motioned for Rubicon, who lifted the light and scanned the slope ahead of him.

"I can't tell where he is anymore," Rubicon confessed. "We'd better head uphill apace." He shoved a bristly pine branch aside and continued up the slope. Soon, the ground leveled off, and they were standing amidst a dense crowd of tree cover, the glow of the lantern barely cutting through the pines. Whatever lay on the far side of the woods was lost to the darkness. Rubicon swung the lamp ahead of him in a slow half-circle, first to his left, then back to his right. He paused, then swung it again—

"Wait!" Elmer hissed. "I see him!"

Rubicon's arm froze, and he held the lantern steady.

Elmer crept forward. "Well, I'll be," he said.

"What?" Rubicon asked.

"There's a clearing up there."

"That's my land!" Rubicon exclaimed.

"Shh!" Elmer hissed, waving a hand behind him. He crept forward another step.

The insects remained silent. In the darkness, only the sound of the men's heavy breathing could be heard. Another long moment passed, thick with the silence of the shrouded woods.

And then, it began.

First, the noise came from somewhere up ahead, far beyond the clearing where Herbert Watkins stood exposed to the elements. But then, it seemed to swirl upward, or perhaps plunge downward from somewhere high. Wherever it came from, the sound was unmistakeable: a high-pitched whine, droning like a hundred humming bumblebees.

Elmer threw up his arms. "Oh no! This is happening too soon. We've got to warn Herbert!" he shouted, springing forward. Before the two men could blink an eye, he had raised his stick, clutched it with both hands, and swung it sideways. Then, he began spinning it end over end, whirling it over and over at a frenzied pace, all the while muttering strange words under his breath.

"Elmer, you crazy loon. What kind of mad plan have you cooked up out here? *And what in tarnation are you doing with that stick?*" Rubicon took a step forward, but stopped as the stick whizzed past his face. He raised the lantern, but Elmer's staff caught it in its orbit, knocking it to the ground with a crash. "Oh, now, that's just great, Elmer. Cut it out!" he hissed.

The whine rose in pitch, growing louder and closer.

"Wings," Wendell muttered. "But that means—"

The din increased. Elmer continued whirling his stick, and Rubicon attempted to get his attention, but to no avail.

Then, from through the trees, the orange glow from Herbert's lantern winked out.

"Oh boy," Wendell muttered.

The whine whirled and swooped, and in the darkness, it seemed to the men that it had taken on a life of its own. But they only stood stupefied until—

"Was that a dog barking?" Rubicon said.

"Fiddlestick!" Elmer called over the deafening cloud of sound. The dog yipped once more, then its voice was lost in the din.

Wendell looked up. "Rubicon, look out!"

But it was too late. Elmer's furious stick-wielding had found another target. Just as Wendell reached out, Elmer's staff connected with Rubicon's head with a mighty THWACK. The bearded man stumbled backward, arms flailing to ward off a second blow. As he did, one fist swung out, finding Wendell's chin. Both men dropped, their heads colliding with each other on their way to the ground.

"Oh no!" Elmer cried. Flinging his satchel from his back, he crouched and pulled out a small jar. He quickly attended to the two men, then leapt to his feet. "Herbert!" he cried. Raising his staff, he charged off through the woods toward the clearing.

As he ran, the whining noise weakened, then ceased completely. But the two men on the ground at the edge of the woods lay still, chests rising and falling in the sleep of the truly exhausted. Or, in this case, the unconscious.

"Rubicon! Come on, fella, get up." Wendell, who had awoken first, crouched beside his fallen friend, shaking his shoulder, which was damp with dew. The blackness of evening was yielding to a dim blue light peering through the trees overhead. Dawn was on its way. Wendell shook him again.

"Wha—who ... Wendell?" Rubicon shook his head once, then sat upright. Instantly, his hand shot to his forehead. "Did I—*did you hit me?*"

"In a manner of speaking," Wendell said. "I believe we both have Elmer to blame for our condition. His staff of protection hit you. And you conked me on the way down."

Rubicon nodded in recognition. Then, a second realization hit him. "Wendell, *what's that smell?*"

Wendell smirked. "I reckon that's the other thing we have Elmer to thank for."

"That's his frog goo, ain't it? He must've smeared it all over us before he took off. " He raised his arm and sniffed. "Wow, is that foul!"

"Sure is," Wendell said. "Look, he even left the jar between us where we fell."

"Thoughtful fella, ain't he?" Rubicon said. "I can't wait to wash this off." His jaw clamped shut and he inspected his arms. "No bites," he muttered. "But it sounded like they were everywhere. You don't think—"

"I see where you're going with this, and I'm not making a guess either way," Wendell said.

"But that noise. Those wings—"

"I know."

"But we don't have a mark on us," Rubicon added.

Wendell shook his head. "I've seen a lot of things in my day. But I've never heard a sound like that. If I was the superstitious kind, I'd say that sound was the most malicious, devastating swarm of—"

"Don't say it," Rubicon said. "You're going to sound like Elmer."

"Well, we don't want that," Wendell said.

"So he ran off after gooping us up with frog guts. But where is ole' Herb?" Rubicon asked, hauling himself to his feet.

Wendell smirked again. "I reckon neither of them waited around much longer to see what happened after we both got our clocks cleaned."

Rubicon winced and rubbed his head. "We've got to get back to town. Wait until I give Elmer a piece of my mind."

"You want to see to the clearing first?" Wendell asked.

"Not particularly. I've seen enough for one day. You lead the way."

And with that, the two men traipsed down the hill, across the damp gully and back up the far side, re-tracing their steps from the night before until they reached Wendell's barber shop. There, in a chair pulled up just outside the front door, sat Elmer Mussel-man. On the ground beside him lay a satchel and a familiar stick.

"Morning, boys," he said. "Glad to see you looking well this morning."

"*Well?*" Rubicon strode up to Elmer, teeth gritted. "I have a nice lump on my head from your trip, and Wendell here might have a loose tooth or two. All because of that crazy mosquito business."

Elmer settled back in his chair and smiled. "But you don't have any bites, do you?"

"That's beside the point," Rubicon said.

"Is it?" Elmer asked.

Just then, there was a commotion from behind Wendell and Rubicon. Both men turned to see Herbert Watkins sprinting across the street toward the shop.

"Would you look at that," Rubicon said.

"Are those—?"

Even in the light of early morning, the great red welts on Herbert Watkins' forehead—and face, arms, and long, spindly neck—were unmistakeable.

"My gracious, Herbert. I don't reckon there's a square inch of you that's un-bitten," Wendell said.

"Fiddlestick," Herbert panted, chest heaving. "Have you seen Fiddlestick?"

"Now hang on, partner, what's this about Fiddlestick?" Rubicon asked, grasping Herbert by the shoulder and steering him closer. He winced as he beheld the dozens of red blotches dotting him like marks on a map. "Did all that happen—"

Elmer placed a hand on Herbert's shoulder. "I tried to get to him in time. But by the time I had attended to you two and reached the clearing, he was covered."

"Covered?" Wendell asked.

Herbert's head bobbed up and down. "They got me. Hundreds of them. Swarming. Swirling. Like a cloud of angry black fire, they were. If Elmer hadn't gotten me out of there … " His voice trailed off.

"Slow down," Rubicon said. "You're saying that—"

"There was that horrible noise, my lantern went out, and they took Fiddlestick!" Herbert shrieked.

"They *what*?" Wendell asked.

"Who?" Rubicon asked.

"The skeeters!" Herbert's voice reached a hysterical pinnacle, his eyes gleaming. "They picked him up and took my Fiddlestick away!"

The two men turned toward Elmer, who merely grinned a cat-with-a-canary sort of smile. "I tried to tell you something was going on up there. Now you know. You've seen for yourself what happens *when the mosquitos sing*."

"I'm not sure we *saw* anything," Rubicon said. "There was that noise, then the darkness. Anything could have happened after that."

Elmer turned to Herbert. "I'm truly sorry not to have reached you in time to prevent your encounter with the skeeters. But I can guarantee you won't be encountering them again. Neither will you, Rubicon."

"What's that mean?" Rubicon asked.

"I've laid protective charms all around that clearing. Your home sweet home up there on Mosquito Ridge will be skeeter-free."

"Oh, is that what we're calling it now?" Rubicon asked.

"Indeed. Of course, those protective charms will wear off. For a small monthly fee, I can keep the super-skeeters away permanently. Shall we talk inside the shop?"

"Monthly fee?" Rubicon said. "You're pushing your luck, Elmer."

"So that's a no?"

"That's a never."

"You'll see," Elmer said. "When you come back, I'll be ready. And I'll even give you a discount, because that's the kind of guy I am."

Herbert's eyes widened. "Would you consider laying some charms around my house?"

"Oh great," Wendell said. He and Rubicon exchanged glances, eyebrows raised. Shaking their heads, they headed to their respective homes for a well-earned hearty breakfast.

And plenty of questions to answer about what exactly had happened up on Kingman Hill the night the mosquitos sang.

THE EDUCATION
OF MISS CAMILLA
WIMBERLY

(1872)

Tucked among the passengers on the west-bound Denver
Pacific rail car that spring afternoon, the petite, brown-
haired woman in the yellow-and-blue checked dress scarcely

attracted anyone's attention. She sat by herself, trading glances between the small book in her lap and the scenery gliding by outside her window.

Those who did notice her, however, might have wondered several things. Why was a woman her age—likely no more than 20 years old—traveling alone on the American frontier? Where was she from? Where was she headed?

But if the woman noticed the occasional sidelong looks, she

didn't acknowledge them. She simply sat with her hands folded in her lap, waiting for the final few miles to pass before the train deposited her in Rattlesnake Junction, Colorado, her new home. She was pretty, with large gray eyes and a dainty, upturned nose. Her hair was mouse-colored and thick, drawn up above her head in a large bun.

Out of habit, she reached into the pocket of her skirt and drew out the folded letter. Though she had nearly committed it to memory since receiving it three weeks earlier, she read it again.

Dear Camilla,

It is with deepest gratitude that I would like to offer you the position of schoolteacher in our humble town of Rattlesnake Junction. You will find the students here a small, but eager bunch, ready for the guiding influence of a properly-trained instructor such as yourself. Their zest for life does lead them—upon rare occasions—to be a bit too boisterous or rambunctious. Yet I have no doubt that, as I mentioned, a well-trained schoolteacher will enjoy such enthusiasm tremendously. Upon your arrival in town, please call upon Patricia Scoggins, and we will see that you get settled in properly. Until then, I remain,

> *Yours in education,*
> *Patricia Scoggins*

"Zest for life" … "A bit too rambunctious" … Miss Wimberly puzzled over those phrases and tried to picture her new brood of

students. A small bubble of anxiety formed in her stomach, but as per her training at the Northeast College for the Teaching Arts, she closed her eyes, balled up her hands, and began counting backward from 10, taking long, slow breaths in through her nose and out through her mouth. By the time she'd reached five, the bubble had nearly vanished.

"See," she said matter-of-factly. "Nothing to be upset about." Returning the note to her pocket, she glanced out the window at the chiseled peaks of the Rocky Mountains and felt her spirits rise. Wasn't this exactly the sort of adventure she had been hoping for when she had first responded to the advertisement in her hometown newspaper in Danbury, Massachusetts?

"You're from hardy farming stock, Camilla," Pa had said, standing beside Ma on the rail platform six days earlier. "There's nothing they'll be able to dish up out there in Colorado that you can't handle." Then, he was off to oversee a large shipment of Roxbury Russet apples. At the memory of her Ma's parting hug, Miss Wimberly could again smell the sweet tang of apples, and a stout wave of homesickness washed her back to the rolling hills and orchards of her family farm. She would miss the farm work, but the thought of growing things in the Colorado soil raised her spirits. Yes, she thought, as the craggy mountain peaks rolled by, she would be up for whatever challenge this new home dished out.

Rowena Bradbury finished her cup of coffee at the Grubstake Hotel and glanced at the clock in the corner. The train was due in twenty minutes. That was plenty of time to make her way across the green, even with the throbbing pain in her big toe. Whatever was wrong with it, it was nothing that a little walking wouldn't fix. Setting three coins neatly on the counter, she stood and hobbled out of the hotel. The afternoon sun was amber, buds were visible on the trees, and the occasional iris and crocus poked its head above the earth. Foot traffic milled about the street in front of the train depot, and the air was refreshingly free of the usual horse or hog-related odors. She couldn't imagine a more perfect spring day to welcome a new teacher to town.

As she moved onto the road, a loud cry echoed across the green. She glanced up to see a ball whistling through the air, directly at her. Instinctively, she dodged, catching her foot on a rock in the dirt and nearly toppling over. As she recovered, three boys raced into sight around Jim-Jay Johnson's elm tree.

"That was a long one. Didn't expect to cork it the way I did!" chirped the first boy, a stout, freckled sort, 12 years old, with a mop of sand-colored hair. He toted a long wooden baseball bat which dragged the dirt behind him as he raced into sight.

"Didn't you hear the crack? I knew you'd gotten all of it, Buck!" A second boy, with round eyes and a wide, round face raced along nearly pace-for-pace with the first boy. Under a cap, his hair was deep brown, and he wore a battered work glove on his right hand.

A third boy loped after them with long, coltish strides, easily able to overtake them, but giving the impression he knew it and thus, was in no hurry. He wore a short-sleeved shirt and dungaree pants, a red bandana tucked into the back pocket.

The trio careened past Mrs. Bradbury, almost as if she was invisible, toward the spot where the ball had rolled to a stop.

"Boys, you'd better watch where you're hitting that ball," Mrs. Bradbury called. "You could really whack someone."

The moon-faced boy turned, a few steps beyond her. "You think so? 'Course, I didn't expect Buck to wallop it the way he did. And if Edgar catches the darn thing ..." His voice trailed off. Mrs. Bradbury was glaring at him, her eyebrows knitted together.

"Ahem ..." she prompted. "What did I just hear, Teddy?"

"I said, if Edgar had caught the ... oh, uh, the blasted baseball, it wouldn't have nearly hit you."

Her gaze remained dark as pitch.

"I mean ... the, uh, ball. Just the, you know, such-and-such ball."

"That's better," Mrs. Bradbury said. "As you know, your language reflects your character. I'm not sure whether Mr. O'Grady taught you that, but you can expect your new schoolteacher will." She paused. "Now, run along and be careful." She wagged her finger at them and turned to leave. But the three boys fell into step beside her as she ambled across the green.

"Did you say *new teacher*?" Buck repeated.

"I did. Direct from Massachusetts, trained at a real teacher college, so you boys had better shape up. No more Homer O'Grady and his lectures on the many uses for corn ..."

"Or his two-hour naps," continued Teddy.

"And his mystery flask!" added Edgar. The three boys elbowed each other hysterically.

"Yes, indeed. None of that," Mrs. Bradbury said flatly. "Now, you carry on with your game." She started off around the green. "But be ready for school bright and early tomorrow. Spread the word!"

The boys watched her leave, then huddled.

"New schoolteacher, huh? Ain't that something?" Buck whispered. "Starts tomorrow, too."

"Are you thinking what I'm thinking?" Edgar asked.

Teddy rubbed his stomach. "I know. But I don't think my Ma's fixing pork cracklings tonight."

Buck smacked Teddy on the back of his head. "You nitwit. I'm thinking we spy on this new schoolteacher. See what we're up against, if you catch my meaning."

Teddy's face cleared. "Oh, ha ha, yeah. That. Me too."

"I can't," Edgar said. "I've got to get home and feed the chickens. Ma was on me something fierce after I forgot yesterday. You go on without me. I'll catch up with you later."

"Alright," Buck said. "I'll stash the baseball stuff and meet you up yonder, Teddy. Be stealthy." He paused. "That means go slow and stay out of sight."

"Ah," Teddy said.

"I guess some of us need the new schoolteacher more than others," Buck muttered, then gathered the equipment and raced away.

Miss Wimberly felt the train jolt to a stop under her. Breathing again through her nose and out through her mouth—though not counting this time—she hefted her trunk off the train and toted it across the apron of the depot. Finally, with her first sight of this new town, she was able to see herself melting into the crowd and making her home here.

Now, to find her host. Scoggins, was it?

"Yoo hoo! Over here!"

Miss Wimberly turned to see a neatly-dressed woman waving at her from across the street. Graying hair peeked from under a lace bonnet, and a lace shawl wrapped her shoulders. She started across the street toward her, limping as she came. "You hoo! Right here, dear!" she called. As she reached Miss Wimberly, her wide brown eyes looked her up and down. "Well, aren't you a petite little thing," she said. "What are you, barely five feet tall?

There's nothing to you. I'm surprised you didn't just blow away on the prairies out there. Ha! And what's that you're wearing? When I heard Massachusetts, I was expecting something a bit more proper."

"Well, I dressed for the trip. As a matter of fact, this is how I always dress."

Mrs. Bradbury's eyes widened, her lips moving slightly. "You do? With that simple dress, and those—are those boots?"

"Yes'm. As I said—"

"Oh no, honey, that won't do. We had one of those country-type schoolteachers, and it didn't work out at all. We need a proper schoolmarm around these parts to whip our youngsters into shape."

"A proper schoolmarm? One of *what* type? I'm afraid I don't understand." Miss Wimberly could feel anxiety rising in her chest. This was not going how she had planned.

"Our former schoolteacher—if you can call him that—was straight from the hills," Mrs. Bradbury continued. "His methods were, ahem, unorthodox, but we let it slide because he was all we could afford. Just when we were getting desperate, he vanished one cold wintry night in late February. For the last six weeks, our poor children haven't had a lick of book-learning. So Patricia Scoggins led the charge and we took up a collection. Folks pledged money, and we put out the call for a real, honest-to-goodness schoolmarm." She leaned toward Miss Wimberly and winked. "That's where you come in. The Northeast College for the Teaching Arts, was it?"

Miss Wimberly's eyes widened. "So you're *not* Patricia Scoggins?"

"Shame on me for not introducing myself. I'm Rowena Bradbury. Mrs. Scoggins will be along shortly, but until then, it's off to Long's General Store so we can get you dressed up nice and proper. None of this country garb. Zip, zap, off we go." With that, Mrs. Bradbury's jaw clamped shut and she steered the wide-eyed schoolmarm up River Street toward Long's General Store.

Thirty-four minutes—and attempts at seven blouses, four bonnets, three hats, and 12 skirts later—Rowena Bradbury and Camilla Wimberly emerged from the general store. They had no idea they were being silently observed by two pairs of eyes, watching from a safe distance behind a cluster of barrels in front of the Silver Dollar saloon.

Two pairs of eyes widened as two jaws dropped.

"*That's* our new teacher?" Teddy asked as they took in the transformed Miss Wimberly. "She's … fancy."

Under Rowena Bradbury's direction, Miss Wimberly looked much less like her true self—a hard-working farm girl from Massachusetts—and much more the part of a proper, college-educated schoolmarm, or at least Mrs. Bradbury's idea of one. She had donned a jet black, high-necked dress with pearl buttons down the front, slim-waisted and covering all but the toes of her matching black-heeled boots. Her dark hair was covered by a fashionable black hat cocked at a rakish angle, several feathers sprouting upward six inches from her head. If an ostrich attended a funeral, it might have dressed like this.

"Close your mouth," Buck answered. "You're going to let in flies." Both boys watched the two women make their way across the green. "This is going to be too easy," Buck added.

"Easy?"

"You know, Teddy, sometimes I wonder how you manage to keep it all together. *I mean*—pulling some of our classic pranks on her will be way too easy."

"You want to get rid of her?" Teddy asked. "But she just got here. And she's … fancy."

"Nah, not get rid of her," Buck said. "I just want to introduce myself properly."

"But this is our last year in school. I've only got a few months left before Pa will finally let me start work on the farm."

"I know. Don't you want to go out with a bang?" Buck asked, grinning.

Teddy smirked and nodded.

At that moment, Edgar appeared beside them. He gathered his breath, wiped his forehead, and crouched. "They didn't see me, I don't reckon anyway," he panted. "What's going on?"

"Buck was just hatching a plan to play some jokes on the new teacher," Teddy said.

"You were?"

"I was."

"So what is it?" Edgar asked.

Buck leaned back, a slow smile stretching across his face. "I was *hatching* it, wasn't I?" He paused. "How were those chickens doing, Edgar? You think they'd be up to traveling tomorrow?"

Edgar's eyes widened, and the conversation continued as three heads now monitored the two women as they paused on the far side of the green. Two new figures moved toward them from the corner of South Street.

"Mrs. Bradbury! I had hoped that was you!" A blonde-haired woman in her late 20's, accompanied by a smaller, nearly-identical version of herself, beamed as she met the pair.

"Why, Patricia Scoggins," Mrs. Bradbury said, "We were just deciding whether to come your way, or head back to my place. This is Camilla Wimberly, our town's new schoolmarm."

"That is quite the professional teacher outfit. They said you were from Massachusetts, but I didn't know that's how teachers were dressing back East."

Miss Wimberly's face flushed. "Well, they don't *all* dress like this," she said.

"This is my daughter, Charlotte," Mrs. Scoggins continued. "She's eight years old."

Charlotte curtsied and held out a folded piece of paper. "I wrote this for you, ma'am. It's a list of all my favorite books."

"She's secretly hoping that you've got a copy of Jules Verne's latest in your classroom library."

Miss Wimberly's face lit up. "*Twenty Thousand Leagues Under the Sea*? As a matter of fact, the voyage of Captain Nemo and his *Nautilus* kept me occupied nearly the entire train trip. What a tale!" she exclaimed.

Charlotte beamed. "You have it!" she squeaked. "I've read *Journey to the Center of the Earth* dozens of times, and—" She leaned forward. "Do you think I could borrow it when you're through?" she whispered.

Miss Wimberly smiled. "Of course."

Mrs. Bradbury raised a hand. "You two can talk adventure stories all night. Miss Wimberly is joining all of us at the Scoggins house for dinner. And, it's customary for the new schoolteacher to find a local family to live with until she gets settled in. I hope it will be alright for you to stay with the Scogginses for a short while."

"It is," Miss Wimberly said. "My trunk is at the general store. I'm sure Mr. Long would deliver it to your house."

"I like your hat," Charlotte said. "It's the prettiest one I've ever seen."

Miss Wimberly's face flushed again. "Thank you, but I didn't really choose—"

Mrs. Bradbury cleared her throat. "She said she believed in establishing a solid first impression, and that's what she's done, hasn't she? Our brand-new Massachusetts schoolmarm." Miss Wimberly frowned slightly. "I'm just glad she's finally here. Lord knows, we needed a change after Homer O'Grady disappeared. What sort of teacher brings his nursing sow into the schoolroom for a lesson?"

Charlotte giggled. "We did learn a lot that day, Ma."

"I bet you did," Mrs. Scoggins said. "Shall we head home, Miss Wimberly?"

They headed down South Street, still being studied intently by the three heads barely visible above the barrels on the saloon porch. Whispers and snickers drifted upward, punctuating a lively strategy session for the following day in the schoolhouse.

A true teacher is first and foremost a learner. She observes her environment, responds to the unique needs of her students, and maintains a firm grip on the reins of the classroom.

The words of Miss Jane Wetherby, chief instructor at the Northeast College for the Teaching Arts, echoed in Miss Wimberly's mind the next morning as she made her way, lantern in hand, toward the school. The sunrise was still an hour off, but, as a firm believer in preparation, she was ready to begin the day. In the interest of goodwill, she had donned the outrageous black dress purchased for her yesterday by Mrs. Bradbury, though it was already feeling a bit tight around the collar. Perhaps she could do away with the hat, at least.

Passing through a stand of juniper trees, she found herself beside a large field surrounded by a split rail fence. Scattered across the field were a dozen large hogs in various positions of peaceful slumber. *A hog pen this close to the schoolhouse?* she thought. *Well, I never.* She made a note to introduce herself to the owner.

She veered left, careful to keep the lantern light from spilling across the pen and rousing the hogs. The outside of the school-house wasn't much to write home about. From where she stood, it was hard to tell whether the building, with its peeling paint and shabby wooden boards, was an extremely large chicken coop, or an extremely small barn. She made her way to the front door, yanking on the handle and receiving a thick cloud of dust in her face. Coughing, she waved away the dust and entered the school-house. As she stepped inside, she gasped.

A shadowy cloaked figure stood silently just in front of her.

"Gracious!" Miss Wimberly exclaimed. Without thinking, she swung hard. Her fist collided, and the figure banged to the ground, then lay still. She took a cautious step forward and nudged it with the toe of her boot. Her boot caught fabric and pulled it away. Underneath was—

"A coatrack," Miss Wimberly said with a sigh of relief. "And a bedsheet. Of course." She chuckled and shook her head, then crouched to set the coatrack upright. "Serves you right for startling me like that." She seemed to recall her older brothers Bobby and Max arranging a similar greeting for their Grandpa Sal in the stables upon his arrival for the Christmas holidays one year. Grandpa Sal had responded by blasting three holes clean through the bedsheet with his revolver.

Their zest for life does lead them—upon rare occasions—to be a bit too boisterous or rambunctious.

Yes, someone had arranged a good old prank as a welcome for her. Smiling to herself, she folded the bedsheet and raised her lantern to make her way toward the front of the room. Miss Wetherby had said pranks were always a popular greeting for boisterous students. And it looked like she had some of those.

How long had the Bradbury woman said it had been since school had let out? Six weeks? It didn't look like a soul had darkened the door since then. A thin layer of dust covered all flat surfaces: the 16 individual wooden desks, the teacher desk at the front of the room, and the top of the small wood stove along the side wall. How long had it been since someone cleaned this room? No matter, she thought, moving to the whisk broom propped in the corner. If she hurried, she could spruce the place up before the students arrived. But first, she needed more light. Fumbling in her handbag, she located the matchbook and lit a pair of lanterns on the shelf in front of her. They hissed to life, and the room took on a bright orange glow.

Instantly, Miss Wimberly's eyes widened at a chalk message written in giant, crooked letters across the board behind her desk.

$$\text{Stay at yer own risc!!!!!!!!!!!}$$
$$\text{from the skoolhous Ghost!!!!!!!!!!!!!!!!!!!!!!!!!!!}$$

She wasn't sure which was more alarming: the message, its spelling, or the ghastly number of exclamation points. Miss Wimberly chuckled as she wiped away the message. Following up the coat-rack prank with a ghostly warning was a nice touch. Whoever was responsible—and she looked forward to meeting them—had a sense of humor. That would work out well, as long as things didn't get out of hand.

At precisely five minutes to eight, daylight streamed through the small windows and Miss Wimberly sat behind her desk making a few final marks in her notebook. The door creaked open, and Charlotte Scoggins entered, accompanied by two small girls, each clutching one of Charlotte's hands.

"Oh, hello Charlotte. I was out of the house before you were up this morning. And I see you have friends with you." Miss Wimberly stood and moved around her desk toward the girls.

"This is Daisy Livingston and Beulah Mae Parker. They're my neighbors. This is their first day in school. *Their Ma and Pa weren't too keen on Mr. O'Grady*," she whispered.

"I see. And how old are you two?" Miss Wimberly crouched in front of the girls.

"I'm Daisy. I'm six," said the girl attached to Charlotte's right hand, her hair sandy and wild.

"So am I. I'm Beulah Mae," said the one on Charlotte's left, rosy-cheeked and pale-skinned, with a crimson ribbon tying back her dark hair.

"Well, I shall do my best to make this a wonderful first day for you both. I have a special spot in the front row, right in front of my desk," Miss Wimberly said.

The two girls both glanced up at Charlotte. "Don't worry," she said. "I'll be two rows behind you, since I'm older." They both nodded. As the three girls made their way across the room, the door opened again, admitting a collection of red-headed children who tumbled over each other into the room. Soon, the riotous amalgam of denim, freckles, and bare feet arranged itself into an odd lineup of five boys.

"Name's Willie A.," said the left-most and shortest, a boy whose mouth barely opened as he answered. "Thirteen. This my last year in school."

"Name's Willie B.," said the next in line, a head taller than his brother. "I'm eleven."

"Name's Willie C.," said the next, taller still. "Nine."

"Name's Willie D.," said the next, shorter than the prior two Willies, but taller than the oldest one. "Seven." A pattern was developing.

"Name's Willie E.," said the final boy, the shortest. "Five. I think." He glanced at his brothers, but they simply shrugged.

Miss Wimberly's jaw fell open. "You're all named Willie?"

Five heads nodded.

"This does present a challenge," Miss Wimberly said.

Five puzzled faces peered back at her.

"What with you all sharing the same name," she explained.

Five faces remained puzzled.

"The name of Willie," she continued.

"How's that?" said the Willie on the left.

"You don't see how that's a problem?" she asked.

"Not 't all," muttered the second Willie. "You want any one of us, just holler 'Willie' and we'll come running."

"Yes, ma'am," said the first Willie. "Makes it a lot easier. Less names to remember and all. That's what Ma always says."

"But what if I just want *one* of you?"

"Suppose you could just holler C," said Willie C. The other four Willies muttered their agreement.

Miss Wimberly nodded. "I see. Hard to argue with that logic, I suppose." She shook her head. "Very well," she said. "You may find your place with the appropriate age group. Youngest in the front row, oldest in the back row, fill in the rest by age. We'll get started in a few minutes. Until then, please open your primers and review your words."

She responds to the unique needs of her students, she repeated, filling in the names of the Willies in their appropriate squares on her seating diagram.

Ten minutes later, the room contained 15 students. Only one desk stood empty, the one in between the two boys who had introduced themselves as Teddy Williams and Edgar Washington, both 12 years old, and also the final two boys to quiet down. There had been quite a bit of whispering to a few of the 13-year old boys seated in the row behind them. Finally, though, all were silent and ready for the first proper greeting from their new teacher.

With a deep breath and a swoop of butterflies in the pit of her stomach, Miss Wimberly glanced up from her seating diagram and began.

"Good morning, class. My name is Miss Wimberly." She paused to write the name in chalk on the board behind her. "And I've come to teach you all the way from—"

CLU-CLU-CLU-CLUCK
CLU-CLU-CLU-CLUCK

A nervous titter of laughter rippled through the room. All eyes swung to the lone window on the right wall. Something was clearly happening outside. But Miss Wimberly continued with scarcely a glance at the window. "As I was saying, I've come to Rattlesnake Junction all the way from a state called—"

CLUCKCLUCKCLUCKCLUCK

The window slid open and a startled chicken plopped through, landing on the floor of the schoolhouse. It blinked and bobbed its head, tail feathers fluttering.

Miss Wimberly narrowed her eyes. Fifteen pairs of eyeballs swung toward her.

CLUCKCLUCKCLUCKCLUCK

Two more chickens fell through the open window and joined their sister on the floor. The clucking intensified. Miss Wimberly moved around her desk and in three strides, reached the small flock of confused hens. She crouched and—

CLUCKCLUCKCLUCKCLUCK
CLUCKCLUCKCLUCKCLUCK

Two more chickens plummeted past her head and landed beside her with a thud. Now, five chickens—Rhode Island Reds if she'd been asked to specify—milled around her on the floor. From behind her, the room was suddenly awash in odd rustlings and shufflings, but Miss Wimberly couldn't take the time to turn and see what was going on. She did the only thing she knew to do. Without a second thought, she scooped up two chickens—both plump young ladies with beautiful cocoa-colored feathers—and tossed them back through the window. A surprised yelp came from somewhere on the other side of the window. Miss Wimberly scooped up the next two chickens and tossed them after their sisters. While she did so, more rustling and scuffling noises came from the schoolroom behind her, along with the sound of a slamming door. Miss Wimberly snagged the final chicken and tossed her out the window, then shut the window, brushed off her skirts, and exhaled.

"There," she said. "That's that."

Sixteen faces stared back at her, wide-eyed.

"Wow," Daisy said from the second row, "Even my Pa can't toss chickens like that."

"Why thank you, Daisy. But—" Miss Wimberly paused. Daisy now sat in the second row, beside Charlotte Scoggins. And in the row behind them sat 13-year old Rebecca Lynn Gillespie, where Teddy and Edgar *had* been sitting before the chickens started arriving. They were now split up, one having moved forward, on the other side of Charlotte Scoggins, and the other backward. And in the second row, two Willies were seated where Miss Wimberly could have sworn two *other* Willies had been sitting. At a desk in the middle of the front row sat a boy she had never laid eyes on before, a stout, curly-haired sort with chubby cheeks and an impish grin on his face.

Miss Wimberly strode back across the room to her desk. Somehow, her seating diagram had managed to vanish. She glanced up at a room hushed with anticipation. The curly-haired boy in the front row, who had to be around 12 years old, was carefully tucking a piece of paper into the pocket of his pants.

She observes her environment, responds to the unique needs of her students, and maintains a firm grip on the reins of the classroom.

Miss Wimberly surveyed the class and breathed deeply in through the nose and out through the mouth, counting backward from 10. When she reached five, she closed her eyes, visualizing the classroom as it was before the chicken prank. Yes, she could see all the students quite clearly. Her memory was one of her special gifts. And in an instant, she knew what was happening, why it was happening, and how best to go about remedying the situation. Panic would not do. Nor would a heavy-handed punishment. She needed to rise above the desk-switching and out the culprits.

"With that interruption behind us, let us begin our lessons immediately, with *no more disruptions*," Miss Wimberly said. *Maintain a firm grip on the reins of the classroom*, the voice in her head reminded her. "Why don't we start with a review of some Colorado geography? When I call your name, answer the question."

The class nodded and shifted in its seats, the room quivering with anticipation at the thought of Miss Wimberly proceeding under the circumstances without her seating diagram.

Miss Wimberly pointed. "Charlotte Scoggins, why don't you start with the capital of our Colorado territory."

"That's easy, ma'am. It's Denver. Pa says it will be a state someday."

"Very good. I hope it will be." Miss Wimberly glanced around. "How about Willie, the tallest peak in the Rocky Mountains?"

Confused expressions flitted across five scattered faces. At their hesitation, Miss Wimberly raised a finger and pointed. "Ah, change that. You there. Roger."

A broad-shouldered 13-year old boy seated in the third row shook his head emphatically. "Nope, I ain't. I mean, I wasn't. I'm Willie, ma'am."

"Which one?"

"Uh, C?"

A boy snorted from the second row.

Miss Wimberly frowned. "You're sure you're not *Roger Smithson?*"

Roger's eyebrows shot up. "Begging your pardon, ma'am?"

"I seem to remember you going by the name of Roger Smithson when you arrived in class." She paused. "You're sure you're Willie?"

The boy's eyes shifted, and he craned his neck toward the chubby-cheeked new arrival in the front row. "Uh, I ... um."

"That's peculiar, indeed, *Willie,*" she said. "Until you can sort out your identity, we'll move on. Let me see. Who will go next? Well, this might be a bit of a difficult question for one so young, but let's see if Beulah Mae can answer one."

At her words, a tiny, dark-haired lass in the fourth row gasped and was immediately shushed by the curly-haired boy beside her, whose name Miss Wimberly remembered being Teddy Washington, formerly of the third row. Teddy clapped a hand onto Beulah Mae's knee. But instead of pointing at her, Miss Wimberly gestured in the direction of the sandy-haired, chubby-cheeked new arrival in the front row. "Now my seating diagram is starting to come back to me. I believe I marked Beulah Mae as sitting in your seat just a moment ago. *Before the chickens arrived.* I'll admit, that's a strange name for a healthy-looking lad like yourself."

"Who? Me, ma'am? I'm—" Buck Carlson gaped. When he had slipped into the room during the chicken distraction, he had simply found the only open desk. It had been vacated seconds earlier when Teddy and Edgar had forcefully relocated the real Beulah Mae to the fourth row.

"Yes, I remember it was definitely Beulah Mae on my seating diagram," she continued. "I can't seem to find it at the moment. Must have wandered off somewhere. Well, Beulah Mae, out with it. The tallest peak in the Rocky Mountains."

The chubby-cheeked boy slumped lower in his seat. "It's Pikes Peak," he mumbled.

"What's that, Beulah? I know your Ma and Pa raised you to speak clearly to your elders. Beulah Mae?" Miss Wimberly leaned forward, a faint smirk twirling her lips as Buck Carlson shifted uncomfortably. "IsaiditsPikesPeak," he blurted out. Then, his jaw clamped shut.

"Very good, Beulah!"

The class erupted in laughter as Buck's face turned crimson. Behind him, two heads—belonging to Teddy Williams and Edgar Washington—swiveled toward each other, and two sets of eyebrows raised in astonishment. Their new Massachusetts schoolmarm had handled the chickens with ease and plowed straight through their desk-switching ruse in less than half an hour flat. The bar had just been raised. And given the situation, new tactics were called for.

"Fellas, the bar has just been raised. This calls for new tactics."

Buck sat squeezed between Teddy and Edgar back of a row of juniper trees at the rear corner of the schoolhouse property. Two hours had passed since Miss Wimberly had turned the prank into a class joke at his expense. As the students fanned out across the grassy field on the far side of the school for their midday lunch and recreation period, the boys could hear calls of "Beulah Mae" echoing toward them.

"Whaddya mean, 'the bar has been raised'?" Teddy asked, stuffing handfuls of raisins into his mouth.

"It means she may be a proper schoolmarm from back East, but she ain't no pushover."

"She *isn't* a pushover."

"That's what I said, Ed. She ain't."

Edgar shoved the remains of a crumbling biscuit into his mouth. "You said 'she ain't no.' And I feel out of respect for her position, you should at least use correct grammar."

"What the—okay, fine. She *isn't a pushover.*"

"Very good. Continue."

"So it's time for us to move to Plan E."

"Plan E?" Teddy asked. "What happened to … you know, the rest of them?"

"We're skipping 'em," Buck said, eyes flashing. "It's time to play for all the marbles."

"Count me in," Teddy said. "So what do we do?"

"Give me a minute," Buck said, peering around the tree at Miss Wimberly. Feathered hat tucked under her arm, she surveyed the children, hand above her eyes to block the gleaming sunlight. He glanced around the field, then stopped and raised his hand sharply. "Aha! I've got just the ticket. But I'm going to need your help, Ed."

"And mine?" Teddy asked.

Buck thought for a moment. "Yeah. Sure. You too. Boys, why don't we take a walk in that direction?" He gestured up the narrow dirt path.

"But that's Mr. McMasterson's hog pen up there!" Teddy said.

"It is, isn't it?" Buck said, a sly smile creeping across his face. "Well, me and Mr. McMasterson know each other fairly well. I don't think he'll mind in the least."

"Mind what?" Teddy asked.

But Buck only smirked and led the way up the path.

"Miss Wimberly," Charlotte called, having left Daisy and Beulah Mae with Rebecca Lynn Gillespie for recreation, "I was hoping maybe we could talk about Jules Verne? You remember, *Twenty-Thousand Leagues Under the Sea*?"

Miss Wimberly turned, still shading her eyes with her hand. "Why, Charlotte, I would love nothing more." She shot a glance over Charlotte's shoulder at the trio of boys creeping away from the schoolhouse. "I believe we might have other matters to discuss as well."

"Where are those boys going?"

"I believe they're headed toward that hog pen over there."

Charlotte's eyes widened. "Mr. McMasterson's hogs! There are a lot of them."

"Indeed. I had hoped the pranking was over, but it seems I've only gotten the boys riled up. This foolishness isn't going to stop, Charlotte. Not without my taking drastic measures, anyhow."

Charlotte nodded. "What do you mean?"

"I believe the boys are about to do something foolish involving those hogs over there. But I think I have just the solution to snuff this little prank war out."

Charlotte smiled. "I'd love to hear more, Miss Wimberly."

"I thought you might. But first, you'll need to run a quick errand into town so your Pa can summon Sheriff Mayberry. And would you mind sparing some of that raspberry jam from your lunch?"

As they advanced up the path, the boys were engaged in a heated argument. While Edgar Washington was making his case that perhaps it was best not to continue to poke the bear, especially when said bear had already proved a worthy foe, Buck Carlson was having none of it.

"It's just sheer, dumb luck. I don't know how she did it, but she isn't actually using any sort of wiles to foil our pranks. She just can't," he protested. "She's from dad-blamed Massachusetts, for crying out loud. She probably sews, takes tea with crumpets every day, and she ain't never been on a horse a day in her life. How can she possibly know anything about frontier pranks?"

He paused. They had reached the corner of the hog pen. The hogs were not asleep anymore. "Give me some of that," Buck said, plucking a strip of dried beef from Teddy's hand and tossing it into the pen. At the presence of food, the hogs began to grunt and jostle each other anxiously.

"I see your point," Edgar conceded. "What's up?"

Buck tossed the remainder of Teddy's beef into the pen and wiped his hands on his pants. "I've been mulling this little beauty of a prank for awhile now, but haven't had the right occasion to get it out. But I think this is the perfect time. There's *no way* she's going to see this coming. You two cover for me while I'm gone. Cause a distraction," he said. "I'll see you back at the schoolhouse in twenty minutes."

Five minutes later, the two boys bolted out from behind the schoolhouse. Miss Wimberly was crouched beside a small boy who sat on the ground, clutching his knee.

"It's alright, Emmanuel. Why don't you just wash it off at the pump over there, and you'll see it isn't much more than a scratch." Emmanuel stood and wobbled to the pump, and Miss Wimberly stood. "Well, hello there, boys. Are you feeling alright today? I don't think I saw you out there for recreation."

Edgar's face flushed. "Oh, uh. 'Fraid I've got a bad case of yellow fever. Just started acting up. Thought I'd sit out."

"Yellow fever?"

"Yellow *spotted* fever," Teddy added.

"Are you sure?" Miss Wimberly's eyes narrowed.

"Well, actually, it's smallpox." Edgar said.

"Smallpox?"

"Uh, he means really *big pox*. They're way bigger than usual," Teddy said.

"I see."

"But Roger Smithson said it should be fine in a day or two," Teddy said. "And his Pa's a doctor. So, don't worry."

"And where's your friend, Buck?" Miss Wimberly asked.

The boys glanced around. "He's not here?" Teddy asked.

"He was here a minute ago," Edgar added.

"I'm sure he'll turn up," Teddy said.

"I declare it sure is sunny out here today," Miss Wimberly said, surveying the field while shading her eyes. "I can't hardly see a single thing. You boys better not go sneaking up on me. I'm liable to jump right out of my skin at the slightest surprise."

The two boys shot each other smirks. "Uh, now that I'm out here on the field, I'm feeling a lot better, actually," Teddy said. "You want to watch us play catch, Miss Wimberly?"

"You've recovered from your *pox*?"

"Yup," Edgar said.

"Totally," Teddy chirped.

"How remarkable," Miss Wimberly said.

"Come watch us," Teddy said.

Over here," Edgar added, jogging across the field away from the hog pen.

"Of course," Miss Wimberly said. She picked up the book Charlotte had left on the grass when she had gone into town, and followed the boys a few paces.

"A little farther," Teddy called across the field to Edgar. "Wait!"

But Edgar had already thrown the ball. And before Teddy could raise his hands, the ball sailed past him and rolled to a stop in front of Miss Wimberly. She stooped and picked up the ball. Edgar held up his hands. "Could you throw it back, ma'am?"

Miss Wimberly smirked. "You boys are baseball players huh? My family back home plays a lot of baseball. Especially on holidays. For our Fourth of July picnic, we have the whole farm turn out for a giant game. Players everywhere. It's a hoot!"

"Farm?" Teddy asked.

"Why, yes," Miss Wimberly said. "My family runs a nice big apple farm in Massachusetts. My whole life, up at dawn for chores, hauling crates, taking care of livestock. It's hard work, but it builds character."

Teddy and Edgar exchanged glances. "That's ... nice, ma'am," Edgar called.

Miss Wimberly cocked her arm, swiveled her hips, and whipped the ball at Edgar. The ball glanced off his hands with a crack and rolled away.

"Holy smokes!" Edgar called. "You put some mustard on that one, Miss Wimberly!"

"Oh, did I? Sorry about that."

Teddy trotted over to Edgar. "When's he gonna get here?"

"I dunno," Edgar said. "Did you see the steam she put on her throw? Maybe we misjudged her."

"What do you mean?"

"Did you hear her? She said she's from *the farm*."

"So?"

"I think she knows exactly what we're up to. We've got to warn Buck!"

"Nah," Teddy said. "You heard him. There's no way she'll see this—"

But at that moment, a panoply of crazed squealing split the air like a pack of fireworks.

Edgar's eyes widened. "Oh no," he said. "Not—"

"The hogs," Teddy finished, whirling to stare at a spot beyond Edgar's left shoulder. Then, Edgar whirled, and both boys' mouths dropped open.

Buck was nowhere in sight. But across the field, careening out of their pen in a display of total pandemonium, were six of Oscar McMasterson's plump, grazing hogs.

But they weren't grazing anymore. Their gate was open, and they were ripe for a charge.

Though earlier in the day the hogs might have looked as sleepy as Everglades alligators, now they blitzed the field like their tails were on fire. Charley McTavish hooted and leaped onto a rock. Althea Bennett dropped to her stomach and lay flat as a board. Little Daisy Livingston shrieked and stood stock-still at the sight of a 120-pound porker barreling down on her. Roger Smithson dashed after her and scooped her up in his arms, leaping aside as the hog thundered past. The rest of the students took similar evasive maneuvers, diving behind rocks and racing around in circles to avoid McMasterson's wild hog herd, who seemed to be relishing their taste of freedom. They made wild, crazed loops around the field. They grunted happily. They rooted their thick snouts into the dirt at every chance they got. They were going, as the expression goes, hog wild.

Edgar and Teddy stood frozen, their backs against the schoolhouse wall, chests heaving.

"Ggggg . . . . Glad we made it out of there in time," Teddy said.

"No kidding."

"Where's Miss Wimberly?" Teddy asked.

Just then, they heard a loud whistle. Miss Wimberly stood astride a large boulder in the center of the field, left arm clutching a thick stick, which she raised overhead like Moses in the face of Pharaoh's army. Bringing her right hand to her mouth, she let loose an ear-piercing whistle. The hogs appeared to collectively flinch, their rampage slowed measurably. Another whistle. More slowing.

Oscar McMasterson appeared at the edge of the field, a pair of black-and-white herding dogs at his heels. He raised his fingers to his mouth and gave his own whistle. The dogs shot forward, snapping at the rear legs of the hogs. In no time at all, the dogs had steered the hogs away from the field, past McMasterson, and into the pen.

McMasterson jogged over to Miss Wimberly. "You know anything about how that gate got open?" he asked. "That could have been real bad."

But before Miss Wimberly could answer, a girl's voice floated across the field to them, raised in a hysterical wail.

"Oh, it hurts, Miss Wimberly. It hurts something awful."

Teddy and Edgar inched away from the building, eyes glued to the field. McMasterson helped Miss Wimberly down from her rock and the two moved toward a small figure huddled on the ground a few paces from the schoolhouse door. The boys moved closer, and their jaws dropped as they saw Charlotte Scoggins writhing on the ground, pain etched across her face. As Miss Wimberly and Oscar McMasterson crouched beside Charlotte, Miss Wimberly leaned close and whispered a few words into his ear. He nodded and glanced around. Miss Wimberly tipped Charlotte's head back, and the students gasped. Something bright and red was smeared across her forehead.

"Oh jeepers," Teddy said. "She's bleeding."

"Yipes," Edgar said.

"Fellas." Out of nowhere, Buck Carlson appeared at the boys' elbows. "Inspecting my handiwork?"

"I think you better see for yourself," Edgar said. "Something went wrong, Buck."

Buck took a step forward, then froze. "Is that …"

"Yup," Edgar said.

"I don't understand. I thought Mr. McMasterson would get them rounded up before anything real bad would happen. But—"

"Look!"

A figure emerged from the woods and strode down the path toward the cluster of children by the schoolhouse door. It was a lumpy man in a tan hat, a gleaming gold star pinned to his shirt.

"Sheriff Mayberry," Buck whispered. "What's he doing here?"

Three heads craned forward.

"Miss Wimberly, I hate to do this, it being your first day on the job and all, but we want you to know we take the safety of our children seriously in these parts. That girl looks badly injured. So while Mr. McMasterson takes her to Doc Smithson, you're going to come to my office to answer some questions."

Miss Wimberly stood shakily. "But Sheriff," she said, her voice suddenly high-pitched and quivering, "I don't know how that happened. I could have sworn that none of the students were playing so close to the hog pen. I just don't know how it happened."

"I understand that, but someone is going to have to answer for the mayor's daughter getting injured."

"Now hang on a minute," McMasterson said. "Let's not get carried away here. Look around. It's all cleaned up. The hogs are away. And this woman didn't have anything to do with it. It was an accident."

The Sheriff raised his hand. "That's enough, Oscar."

"Will I be able to keep my job? Will I?" Miss Wimberly's voice climbed higher.

"I can't say, ma'am," Sheriff Mayberry said. "I can't say."

Miss Wimberly's shoulders slumped, and she trudged off under the watchful eye of the sheriff. Oscar McMasterson scooped up Charlotte Scoggins and followed them down the road to town. The students watched them leave, and a few sniffles could be heard.

"I didn't think this would happen," Buck said to the two other boys. "I didn't think so many would get loose. And I definitely didn't think they'd hurt anyone. And for Miss Wimberly to take the blame for it …" His voice trailed off.

"We've got to do something about it," Edgar said. "You've got to tell the Sheriff what happened."

Buck frowned. "But if I do that—"

"You heard him, she could lose her position for this. You said it was all in good fun. It's gone too far, Buck."

Buck nodded. "I reckon it has."

"Let's go," Teddy said.

The three boys edged down the wall, then took off at a sprint for town.

Six minutes later, the door to the sheriff's office flew open, and three boys tumbled inside. They blinked at the empty room. A cat glanced up at them from the desk, raised one eye, and stretched lazily.

"What? I don't get it," Buck said between heavy breaths. "They were … coming here … right?"

"Uh huh," Edgar said.

"Then where are they?" Buck asked. He peered into the next room. The sheriff's desk, too, appeared to be vacant. But sitting on the edge of the desk was a small metal lunchbox. He picked it up and swung the lid open. Inside was a crumpled ball of wax paper and a mostly-empty jar of raspberry jam.

Blood-red raspberry jam.

Buck's eyes narrowed. His lips began to move. But as they did, he noticed for the first time that the sheriff's chair sat swiveled away from him, and it was not unoccupied.

CREEEEEEAK

Buck lunged forward, dropping the lunch pail. "Sheriff! It was me. I opened the gate. Those hogs got loose because of me. I didn't intend for Charlotte Scoggins to get hurt or nothing. I just wanted to have a little fun with the new schoolmarm. That's all. You got to believe me. I never meant for her to lose her position or get arrested or nothing like that … Sheriff? Sheriff … ?"

The chair swiveled fully around to face him.

"Why, hello Buck."

Buck's mouth dropped open. Miss Wimberly grinned and straightened the fancy black hat atop her head. "You reckon we can commence with your education now?"

Buck's eyes bulged. So did Teddy Williams' and Edgar Washington's. Three mouths gaped as Miss Wimberly gestured, and a remarkably un-bloody Charlotte Scoggins crawled from her spot behind the desk. Sheriff Mayberry and Oscar McMasterson entered the office through the front door.

"You were all in on it?"

Miss Wimberly nodded, smiling. "Well, not at first."

"This girl came into my office around the lunch hour to ask if I would come up to the schoolhouse and play my part in helping you boys learn your lesson about, ahem, knowing your boundaries," Sheriff Mayberry said.

"And once I got the hogs rounded up, Miss Wimberly kindly informed me what you boys were up to," Oscar McMasterson added. "Those old hogs get tired pretty easily. It was dangerous for a minute or two there, but they'd have run themselves out in no time. *Not that I appreciate you setting them loose,*" he added, glaring at Buck, who gulped.

"You've got to get up pretty early in the morning to pull one over on a farm girl like me," Miss Wimberly said. "I didn't expect my first day to come to this, but after the morning we had, it was going to take drastic measures." She paused. "You suppose we can settle down now and do some proper learning?"

Three heads nodded.

Sheriff Mayberry clapped a hand on Buck's shoulder. "I believe that's going to be the end of your time in school, boys. I know for a fact that each of your fathers could use a pair of willing hands to help with the chores."

Miss Wimberly stood. "Actually, I'd like for them to stay in school for a few more months, Sheriff," she said. "I know it might not be my place to decide, but I like 'em. They've got spirit. I'd like to see their time in school be memorable. *For the right reasons.*"

Sheriff Mayberry nodded. "That sounds fine with me. I don't rightly care too much either way. I was only thinking of protecting you from—"

Buck squirmed out from under the Sheriff's hand. "Begging your pardon, sir. But I don't think Miss Wimberly needs any protecting. Golly, I don't think so." And three boys breathed three sighs of relief, as they saw their first day in Miss Camilla Wimberly's classroom come to a rousing conclusion with a lesson in respect they wouldn't rightly forget in a month of Sundays.

Four days later, the Rattlesnake Junction Board for the Betterment of the Educational Situation of the Youth met in the parlor of Rowena Bradbury's house to discuss the week's events. The meeting sailed along smoothly, accompanied by slices of Minnie Gillespie's strawberry-rhubarb pie. Just as Mrs. Bradbury was preparing to adjourn, Mrs. Scoggins raised her hand.

"Just one more item, if you please, Rowena." She stood, raising a slender brown-paper package and motioning toward Miss Wimberly. "I can't begin to say how sorry we are that your first day here in Rattlesnake Junction turned out the way it did, Camilla," she said.

Miss Wimberly smiled. "I really think you all are making too much of a fuss about this. I'm a teacher, and that's what I signed up for: guiding and shaping the lives of young people."

"Be that as it may," Mrs. Scoggins said, "we all chipped in to give you a little token of our gratitude. My Charlotte said you like to supervise the children when they're at recreation time, but you often find the sunshine on that open patch of land a bit too harsh. Now that you've given up wearing that ridiculous hat"—she winked at Mrs. Bradbury—"we hope this remedies that problem." She handed the parcel to Miss Wimberly, who unwrapped it to find a sturdy wooden umbrella, as bright and yellow as a daffodil. "It's our hope you will use this umbrella in—what did you just call it—the 'guiding and shaping of young people.' Will this help?"

Miss Wimberly smiled. "Yes, I believe this will certainly help. Thank you all so much."

"Terrific. Rowena?"

"Again, I'm terribly sorry about the misunderstanding about Massachusetts," Mrs. Bradbury said. "I think we've all learned something this week. Shall we adjourn?"

Just then, there was a knock on the parlor door. It opened to admit the handsome figure of Mayor Avery Scoggins, a bashful smile on his face. "Very sorry to interrupt, ladies, but I wanted you to be the first to hear the news. Based on the success of our investment in education, the town board has decided that we should go in search of a proper preacher. The church is growing, and it needs some leadership of its own.

"Matter of fact," he continued, "we've got a lead on a preacher from Kansas City. I believe he goes by the name of Elijah Appleton. He's got a tremendous wife named Ruth and a son about my daughter Charlotte's age." He paused. "Can't seem to remember the boy's name right now. No matter. We'd like to try get the preacher installed before summer is out. What do you all think of that?"

DEAD-EYE DAN
AND THE
LARAMIE SEVEN

(1875)

By Sean Douglas McCaskill
As read by Eugene Appleton

The moon overhead would have been as round as a dinner plate, and it would have gleamed a perfect disk of white light onto the outstretched palm of Dan Crowley that cool August evening.

But there was no moon. And Dead-Eye Dan had a sneaking suspicion that was going to be important.

Crowley, the ace sharpshooter and U.S. Marshall, stood outside a rustic cabin in the deserted wilds of Utah, thirty miles from anywhere. The cabin looked empty.

But Dead-Eye Dan knew better.

Inside the cabin were four of the frontier's most notorious outlaws, a gang known as the Laramie Seven. True, there were no longer actually seven members of the Laramie Seven, and true, they were a long way from Laramie right now, but that's the thing about a name. Once a moniker's attached to you, it's stickier than a lizard's tongue. Dead-Eye Dan Crowley knew that better than most. At seven, he had won the Muskogee County Fair sharp-shooting contest. At twelve, he'd bested a hundred men twice his size at the Oklahoma State Fair by punching a hole through a target at a distance of three hundred feet.

And now, at thirty-two, you'd be hard-pressed to find a single man with a Winchester anywhere in the entirety of the United States who could wield a rifle with any more accuracy than Dan Crowley. Thus, "Dead-Eye."

But right now, he wasn't Dead-Eye Dan Crowley. He'd set that name down in favor of a new one: Winston Rafferty, a down-on-his-luck drifter with a checkered past. Rafferty had happened to not-so-coincidentally bump into the Lararmie Four—er, Seven—six months earlier. Gone was Crowley's silver Marshall's star. Gone was his wedding ring. Gone even was Alejandro, his faithful Winchester rifle. All had been set aside when he had begun this undercover job.

Now, after dozens of twists and turns, something big was about to happen. Dead-Eye Dan didn't know where. He didn't know when. But he would be ready when they told him. And then the axe would fall. The Laramie Seven would be brought to justice.

Dead-Eye Dan pressed his ear to the front door of the cabin. All was quiet, except for one low voice speaking with flinty resolve. Crowley raised his hand and cracked his knuckles against his weathered cheek. Then, he rapped on the door. *Rat-tat.* Pause. *Rat-tat-tat-tat.* Pause. *Rat-tat-tat.* Pause.

The voice inside stopped. The sound of footsteps drew closer to the door. Crowley lowered his hand. He was about to enter the lion's den for the final time. And he had naught but his wits to guard against the hungry beasts within. If anything went wrong—

The door creaked open, and a man stepped out, his face shrouded in shadow. The man reached for his gun belt. Dead-Eye Dan flinched, but he forced himself to wait, feeling the hairs on the back of his neck prickle. The hand paused on the gun handle, then relaxed.

"Yer late," the voice growled. "I don't take kindly to tardiness as a quality in my partners. Makes me suspicious." The man stepped back, allowing Dead-Eye Dan to pass through the doorway ahead of him. Light from the cabin revealed his features for the first time: a thick, bristly mustache, wizened features on a deeply-creased forehead, and the tip of his left ear gone, shot clear away by U.S. Marshall Stephen Walker in a raid nine months earlier. It was the raid that had led to this very assignment. What remained of the ear belonged to none other than Sal Brinkman, the Lizard of Laramie. No one knew what Sal was short for, but there was plenty of speculation over whether it was short for "salamander." One thing was certain: Sal Brinkman was as cold-blooded a cattle rustler as the Wyoming territory had ever seen. Hence, the "Lizard of Laramie."

"Sorry, sir. Won't happen again." Dead-Eye Dan's voice raised a half-octave, and he began the telltale fidget that had been his defining characteristic when he created the role of Winston Rafferty.

"Sure as spitting it won't. Now get in here." Brinkman waved Dead-Eye Dan inside, where he slid into a wooden chair against the wall. Dead-Eye Dan's gaze made its way around the room of the small cabin, catching the eyes of Walt Calloway and Roddy Jensen, two of the other three members of the Laramie Gang. Where was George Haverhill? he wondered. Easing back in his seat, he tipped his hat to the other men. It had taken a lot of hard work, but he had eventually won their acceptance. Now, he was above suspicion; he was sure of that. Still, there was something in the way Sal Brinkman's eyes seemed to look past Dead-Eye Dan, even while he was staring right at him, that made Dan the slightest bit edgy. Dead-Eye Dan was a master of reading people, but even he couldn't quite translate the Lizard of Laramie.

Dead-Eye Dan removed his hat, leaned back, and listened.

"So it's all settled, then?" Brinkman wandered idly around the room, then stopped at the seat across from Crowley, where Calloway, the fastest rider in the group, sat. He had been tasked with reconnaissance that morning.

"That's right. I saw it with my own eyes. The herd is up on the hillside, and he grazes them pretty consistently. Should be as easy as nicking penny candy from the bin." He chuckled and elbowed the wiry man to his left, who sat unblinking, his hands tying and untying a length of rope. "Right, Jensen?"

Jensen smirked and tightened the rope. Calloway's chuckle grew louder.

Brinkman's eyes narrowed. "Ain't nothing easy, in my experience." His tongue flicked in and out from between his lips, and he raised his hand slightly. The laughter died away. Brinkman turned toward Dead-Eye Dan. "Rafferty, I'm hoping you've got a mighty helpful weapons report for us."

"The rifles are all in perfect working order. I gave them each a cleaning and rubdown this afternoon. We've got plenty of ammunition, enough to go after the entire U.S. Cavalry, I reckon. Had to do a little persuading of the gentleman in town to get him to give me that much. But, eventually, he came around."

"You went into town?" Brinkman's tongue flicked out again.

"Yeah, that's why I'm back so late. Don't worry. There's no way he could trace us out here, with no moonlight. And I doubled back on myself twice to throw anyone off, just like you taught me." Dead-Eye Dan had to fight back a smirk at the thought of timid "Winston Rafferty" having to be taught to double back his horse to cover tracks. But it was all part of the game, he thought, and he was playing it quite well.

Sal Brinkman studied Dead-Eye Dan's face, his tongue again flicking in and out of his mouth. Finally, he relaxed. "Well, I reckon that's good news. We might need it tonight. With that taken care of, let's move out."

Dead-Eye Dan's eyes widened. "Tonight?"

Brinkman cocked his head. "I decided to move up the time-table, take advantage of the first moonless night. Hope that's alright with you," he added sharply.

"Right. Of course." Dead-Eye Dan nodded briskly, cursing his reaction. Winston Rafferty wasn't supposed to be the sharpest tool, but that had been a slip-up, he could tell. He studied Brinkman's face, but it revealed nothing.

"We ride east, ten miles to the ranch, and then the rest of the way to Salt Lake City," he said. "The five of us can keep that herd together for the twenty miles or so until we get there, s'long as we find the trail. Don't want to run into the salt lake itself, mind you."

Dead-Eye Dan nodded to himself. The salt lake. A legend in the American frontier. He'd never ventured this far west in the Utah territory, but he'd heard about it from nearly every trader and trapper he had encountered. A vast inland lake, as wide as the ocean, but with no tide. He almost wished they weren't traveling by night. What a sight to behold.

Feeling the other three members of the Laramie gang's eyes fixed on him, Dead-Eye Dan turned, slipping back into character.

"The ammunition is in a crate beside the house. I'll distribute it into the saddlebags and meet you outside."

Brinkman's eyes remained narrowed, and he barely nodded as Dead-Eye Dan slipped outside. On the front step, he loosened his red bandana. He suddenly felt warm all over, sweat prickling the back of his neck. That had been too close. At this point in the game, every move had to be calculated, every step perfect. One slip, and—he couldn't finish the thought.

Instead of moving to the ammunition chest, Dead-Eye Dan took off into the darkness. He ran flat-out for fifty yards until he reached a small paddock. At the noise of his approach, the slumbering horses began milling about the narrow enclosure, whinnying and stamping. But Dan moved swiftly to the horse nearest the gate, the one he'd ridden back from his evening mission.

The one that hadn't been there earlier.

Clambering over the fence, he swung himself directly from the top rail onto the bare back of the horse. With practiced ease, he guided the horse backward a few steps. Then, he muttered a few words to the horse and dug his heels into the horse's flank. It leapt ahead, reaching a trot almost instantly as it raced across the paddock. Dead-Eye Dan pressed himself nearly flat against the powerful horse's back as it sailed over the top rail of the fence.

"Yaaaa!" Dan hissed, careful to keep his voice to a whisper. "Atta boy, Whirlwind!" He squeezed hard with his left thigh, and

Whirlwind responded, veering left up a slope. They raced across the ridge for a scant moment, before plunging back down the other side. At the bottom of the ravine, Whirlwind came to a stop. Dead-Eye Dan dismounted and placed his hands against the big horse's flank. "Stay here. I'll be right back." The horse raised its head and snuffled gently. "Thanks, buddy," Dead-Eye Dan said, slipping around Whirlwind. He stopped a dozen paces from the far wall of the ravine, raised his fingers to his lips, and gave a short, high-pitched whistle. *Too-wheeeet, to-wheet.* Dead-Eye Dan paused, scanning the shadowed landscape for any trace of movement. Long seconds passed, and Dan raised his fingers to his lips again.

A figure stepped out from behind a rocky outcropping. Instantly, Dead-Eye Dan's hand shot to his empty belt, but remembered too late that Rafferty had asked for his holsters. His realization was followed instantly by a sound he knew all too well: the hammer of a Colt revolver clicking into place.

"The fourth man," he muttered to himself, cursing himself for the second—but not the final—time that fateful day.

"Stay right where you are, Winston Rafferty. Or should I call you Dan Crowley?" The voice was like a piece of sandpaper being drawn across a pine board.

"George Haverhill," Crowley said. "That's why you weren't at the cabin."

"You're correct. Had a few things to settle up out here first.

Like locating your deputy, for example. When were you supposed to meet him? Or was he just out here waiting for you, so you could spill the beans on us?"

Crowley's jaw tightened, and he cracked his knuckles against his cheek. "Haverhill, if you've done anything with Charlie, I swear you'll rue the day you ever laid a scummy finger on him."

Haverhill stepped from the shadows, holding aloft a small branch swaddled in a rag. He wedged the makeshift torch into a crack in the rock, then drew out a match, which he lit and raised to the torch. Soon, the tip of the branch was ablaze, and Dead-Eye Dan could see every ounce of malice gleaming in the thin man's dark eyes.

"Oh, you're worried about him, are you?" Haverhill sneered. "If I was you, I'd be much more worried about your own hide right now, Crowley. You tangled with the wrong group of fellers."

"Is that so?" Crowley's lips parted in a wry smile. "And I suppose you're going to come over here and take me back to the cabin with you?"

"No, he ain't. We all are." A voice boomed out from behind Dead-Eye Dan. He whirled, and a flicker of Haverhill's torchlight brought another face to him.

Sal Brinkman.

"Well, that changes things, doesn't it?" Crowley muttered. "Gee whiz, Whirlwind, things just keep getting grimmer and grimmer."

Brinkman threw back his head, teeth gleaming in a crooked smile as he laughed long and loud. Dead-Eye Dan wasn't watching, though. Dead-Eye Dan was planning. But before he could devise a crackerjack escape, a shot rang out. A chunk of rock spat into the air, inches from Dead-Eye Dan's shoulder.

"Oh, no you don't," Brinkman called. "I know what's going on in that head of yours, and if you think we're giving you enough time to scheme, you've got another thing coming, old boy." He paused. "Haverhill?" he called.

Crowley turned just in time to see the barrel of a pistol whizzing through the air. He raised his arms, but the gun collided with his skull, and he felt himself crumple to the ground. Then, night took over, and his eyes gave way to the blackness.

Chick-a-dee-dee-dee. Chick-a-dee-dee-dee.

The bird call shook Dead-Eye Dan from sleep, and the Marshall's eyes fluttered open. A chunk of sleep wedged itself into the corner of his eye, and he moved to wipe it away.

"What the—rope?" he mumbled. And then, he remembered. And his eyes popped open.

He found himself staring up at a cloudless blue-gray sky. Morning had dawned, and by the look of the light, it was nearing six o'clock. He lay flat on his back, arms roped behind him, hat low over his forehead. With a few quick movements, his hat slid off, and with another few quick movements, he had rolled to his side. The ground below was tight-packed dirt, of a sort that Crowley had never seen. The consistency was fine, tiny grains which slid from his clothes as soon as he came in contact with them.

"Can't be ..." Dead-Eye Dan rolled himself over again, nearly face down this time, and stuck out his tongue. Closing his eyes and pressing his face downward, he drew back almost as soon as his tongue touched the ground. He wiped his tongue against his shirt sleeve. So that confirmed it.

"Salt," he muttered. "What in the blue blazes is a chunk of salt doing out here in the ..." But his voice trailed off again. With each passing moment, the light of dawn brought more of the barren country into view. He raised his head and squinted into the distance. The dirt ahead was white. Bone white. Skeleton white. Only a small, scummy pool lay a few feet away from him, its surface dotted with insects. So much for fresh water.

Crowley shook his head. "A field of salt," he said. "Gee whiz, that ain't a good spot to find yourself in." He threw himself onto his back again, and went to work on the ropes. Setting aside the few bare facts circling his head like buzzards, he attempted to concentrate all his attention on slithering out of Brinkman's knot. But as his fingers dug into the thick cord of the rope, he felt his concentration slipping. The facts resumed circling:

1) Based on the sunset yesterday, it was going to be hot today. Probably close to one hundred degrees.
2) Nothing sucked moisture out of you like salt.
3) The Laramie gang had left him miles from anywhere.
4) With nothing except his hat.

"Gee whiz, this surely ain't a good spot to find yourself in," he repeated, continuing to work the knot. Finally, Dead-Eye Dan felt the ropes slide loose. He kicked at them like they were angry snakes, stomping a few times for good measure. Then, he turned and took in the scene before him. A lesser man might have sat and cried into his handkerchief at the sight of the miles and miles of salt plains ahead of him.

But Dead-Eye Dan wasn't crying. Dead-Eye Dan was planning.

He scooped up his hat and plunked it onto his head, sliding his bandana onto the back of his neck. His knife was gone from his ankle sheath. Of course, his knife was gone. What kind of outlaws would they be if they'd left Dead-Eye Dan a trace of hope in this barren wilderness? He rummaged inside his pockets. A mild break. They'd forgotten to check his pockets. But all he could find inside was a hand's length of twine, a needle, a candy wrapper, a few copper nickels, and a cork.

If the gang had been successful, they'd have rounded up the cattle by now and were headed toward Salt Lake City. He had no way of knowing how far away he was. But he had to start moving east.

Glancing up at the hazy sun, Dead-Eye Dan turned once to check his bearings. Then, he turned again. By the time he had spun around twice, he knew he couldn't count on the hazy sky for direction. He plunged his hands back into his pockets. Some scrap of an idea lay inside his head like the needle and change in his pocket.

Like the needle …

His head shot up. Pulling out the contents of his pockets, Dead-Eye Dan moved to the small pond and deposited his stash of detritus on the salty ground. He glanced up at the sky, praying this would work. Then, he reached for the hem of his shirt. Finding a loose thread, he stripped it away from the shirt, inch by inch, until he could see a thin, eight-inch thread in his palm. Lifting the needle, he began to rub it end to end against the thread, back and forth, the tip of the needle pinched hard between the thumb and forefinger of his left hand, the thread in his right. Finally, after several minutes of this sliding, Dead-Eye Dan set down the thread and reached for the cork. He laid the cork in the shallow pool, waiting a moment while it bobbed, then rested still.

Then, the moment of truth.

Holding his breath, Dead-Eye Dan lowered the needle and set it gingerly atop the cork. Then, he inched his hand away, breath still caught in his throat. His eyes were glued to the cork, and he waited.

The cork began to drift, making a slightly clockwise rotation.

At first, it was barely noticeable, but Dead-Eye Dan waited until the cork had rotated nearly a quarter-turn. Then, it stopped.

Dead-Eye Dan's eyes widened.

If he'd managed to magnetize the needle, when its movement stopped, it would be facing north. And it had stopped.

"Thank you," he whispered. He glanced up and peered into the distance. There, almost on the edge of the horizon, he could glimpse the faint outline of a single, gnarled tree. His heart leapt as he saw it. From the location of north, the tree stood nearly due east. He had his heading. So east he would go. He plucked the cork and needle from the pool and pointed his boot tips due east.

Boots scuffing the hard-packed salt, Dan set off across the vast plain toward the tree. As he hiked, his mind whirled, coming to rest on Charlie, his faithful deputy. He hadn't been at the meeting spot. What did that mean? Had Brinkman actually done away with him, or had that been a bluff? Maybe Charlie had sniffed out the double-cross and, with no way to contact Dead-Eye Dan, simply called off the meet-up and vamoosed.

The heat began to sink deep into him, and Dead-Eye Dan could feel the sweat beading on his forehead. He tugged on the brim of his hat and focused all his attention on the stark white landscape before him. His legs pumped powerfully, and by the time an hour had passed, he had cleared four miles. After two hours, another four. His shirt had been soaked through for some time, and his bandana had become a warm rag. As the close of hour number three came into sight, his confidence began to flag. He felt as though he'd been dropped onto the surface of some foreign, lifeless planet. He could be walking for days, with no change. This was lunacy!

He smacked his hand hard against his thigh. This was what happened. The odds grew longer, and weaker men grew … well, weaker. But it wouldn't happen to Dead-Eye Dan. People were counting on him. His country was counting on him. He couldn't let the Laramie gang get away.

All the same, though, he could feel the unmistakeable throbbing in his temples, the dull ache which began in the small of his back and crept up his spine until it reached the base of his skull. There was no denying it. Dead-Eye Dan was fading by the minute. He needed water. And he needed it soon.

Glancing up toward the sun, nearly at its apex, he fumbled with his shirt buttons, undoing the top two and feeling the air against his bare chest. A moment of relief, followed shortly by the same prickle of heat he'd been feeling for hours. Without a breeze, any trace of relief was fleeting.

But then, as he raised his head and peered into the distance, through the shimmer of heat, he saw …

Water?

He blinked once, rubbed his eyes, and felt his pulse quicken. A minute passed, and he dared himself to squint again at the blur in the distance. It was water. Not an illusion playing tricks on his desperate eyes. Actual water. His tongue scraped the roof of his mouth at the thought of a cool drink. He broke into a jog, feeling his leg muscles protest as he ran. The salt gave way to rock, and the ground sloped downward as he reached a wide, rocky shore. Clambering over a pile of rock, Dead-Eye Dan stopped, stupefied at what he saw.

Before him lay a lake, water lying still against the shoreline. There were no waves, and instead of the sand of a beach, he saw the white-yellow crust of heaps and heaps of accumulated salt.

Salt.

The weight of the realization slammed against Dead-Eye Dan's back like a whip, and he limped forward to the edge of the lake. Dipping a hand down, he brought the warm water to his lips, then spat it back out as soon as it reached his tongue.

Salt water. Utterly undrinkable.

Dead-Eye Dan crumpled backward, the heat of the sun now boring into him like an auger into soft ground. He had no plan. The day was slipping away, and with each minute, he was losing his grip on the Laramie Seven. His options were dwindling by the second. But first, he had to get out of the sun.

Struggling upward, he clambered like a fox into a small crevice nestled beneath an overhang of rock a few yards away. He gritted his teeth. This was no time for weakness. He would make a plan. There was always a plan. But what? He slumped against the rocky wall of the small crevice, feeling a wave of dizziness sweep over him. He closed his eyes. The blistering sun shimmered even in that darkness. But then—

Plop

The slightest sound, but still audible. He opened his eyes and saw a single droplet of water dangling from the lip of the rock beside him. It hung there for a second, then fell loose and plopped to the ground. In its place, a second drop formed.

Dead-Eye Dan's eyes widened.

A plan.

He leapt into action. Jogging out of his hiding spot, he emerged into the brilliant sunlight, glancing around for the right spot. Then, he spied it—up the shore, no more than 50 feet: a long, deep stretch of dirt in between the rock and the salt of the shore. He ran to it, his heart thudding, and threw himself to his knees in the dirt. Then, he began to dig. With nothing but his hands for a shovel, Dead-Eye Dan flung dirt away, down and down, until finally, he reckoned that he'd cleared away enough dirt to leave two mounds. They protruded from the dirt like camel humps, each a foot tall and nearly as far apart.

Satisfied he'd gotten the depth right, Dead-Eye Dan trotted up the slope and found a heap of loose rocks. Smashing them into smaller stones, he hefted three melon-sized ones and carried them back to the spot where he'd dug the holes and raised the pillars. He scraped some dirt from the backside of the first pillar, then gingerly wedged the three rocks into place. He returned to the pile of rock and removed several more, returning to the second small pillar of dirt and repeating the process of wedging the rocks into the side of the pillar. Though nothing had been accomplished yet, Dead-Eye Dan could feel hope stirring in his chest. This thing he'd built might just stand a chance at working. But, first—

Dead-Eye Dan moved to the space directly between the two pillars. He knelt between the two humps and scraped a smaller mound of dirt together. In the center of this little pillar, he scooped out a hollow, like a shallow pool, without the water. Which, Dead-Eye Dan thought with a wry smile, was exactly what it was. In between the center pillar and the two larger ones, he scooped out two more small hollows, little openings ready to hold water.

He stood and whipped off his shirt, wincing as the sun slammed into his bare torso. He stretched out the shirt, wrapped one arm over the top of the left pillar, and placed the pile of rocks on top. Then, he repeated the process with the second arm of the shirt and the second pillar. He grabbed one final rock and placed it gingerly in the middle of the shirt, suspending it directly above the small altar. The shirt sagged slightly in the center, but did not fall. Dead-Eye Dan nodded his approval. Only one item was left.

Taking a deep breath, Dead-Eye Dan removed his hat and set it upside-down in the small hollow he'd made in the center pillar. He glanced down again at the small amount of water that had seeped into the two ground-level crevices under his shirt. He needed more water. Plucking his hat from its resting place, he moved to the lake, crouched and scooped up a hatful of salt water, then dumped it into the small pools. He repeated the process until the crevices were full of salt water.

When he finished, Dead-Eye Dan stood back, arms crossed, and inspected the apparatus. Though rudimentary, it stood a chance of accomplishing its purpose. But it would take time. He must be patient. How much time did he have?

Glancing up at the sun again, Dead-Eye Dan guessed it was nearly noon. He'd gotten quite skilled at gauging time from the position of the sun from White Tail, his guide. Patience, he told himself.

So, as the first beads of fresh water began to form on the underside of the shirt, Dead-Eye Dan staggered back to his shelter. Drumming his fingers nervously on the rock, he settled in to wait. Seconds turned to minutes, and he licked his dry tongue over his lips. Also dry.

This was as bleak a situation as Dead-Eye Dan could ever remember having stumbled into. But he had to stay positive. Once he got out—not *if*, he reminded himself—he could still salvage the operation. It would mean moving at blinding speed, across unfamiliar terrain, but he could do it. If—

There he went with *if* again. His thoughts were becoming as loose and swirling as the hazy sky above him. But even now, as he stared at the lake, he could have sworn there was something atop it, a fuzzy sort of shape walking on it. But Dead-Eye Dan couldn't bring himself to raise his head from where it rested against the rock wall. He would close his eyes, only for a second or two. The hazy figure drifted closer, his eyelids fluttered, and—

Chick-a-dee-dee-dee

Chick-a-dee-dee-dee

Dead-Eye Dan sat bolt upright with the sound, his heart thudding in his chest. "Gee whiz, I must have nodded off where I sit, smack in the middle of the day," he said to himself. He rubbed a hand across his weathered cheek. He knew what was happening. He'd been without water for half a day, had lost goodness-knows how much through perspiration. The dozing off, the vision in the water—if his plan didn't work ...

Shoving himself backward against the rock, Dead-Eye Dan began the slow task of hoisting himself to his feet. He struggled upright, shook himself a few times, and moved out of the shade toward the apparatus he'd built. He could feel his muscles tense as he approached. Would it work?

As Dead-Eye Dan reached the center pillar and bent over his battered brown hat, he felt his spirits rise. The bandana was saturated with water. As he watched, a single droplet, then another—just like the ones he'd seen dropping from the rock a short time earlier—plunged downward into the waiting receptacle of his hat.

Into the *small pool of fresh water* which now lay inside his hat.

"Gee whiz, it worked!" Dead-Eye Dan hooted, showing more emotion than when he'd encountered the all-you-can-eat pancake special at that inn outside Reno. He leaned forward, careful not to disturb the bandana, and slid his hat out. Then, in a moment as glorious as he had hoped, he tilted the brim, cupping it slightly, and let the water trickle down his throat. For three long seconds, Dead-Eye Dan felt the clear, fresh water—warm, of course, but still fresh, not salty—slide down his parched, ragged throat.

Then, he swallowed. In an instant, he could feel his spirits revive. The haze inside his head began to drift away. It had only been a few swallows, but hallelujah, he felt like a new man. Imagine what would happen if he waited even longer?

And so, he did.

There on the shore of that awesome lake of salt, Dead-Eye Dan Crowley waited like a schoolchild patiently anticipating lunch time, as the minutes crept by, until he was sure his battered old hat had collected sufficient water. Then, he returned to his small altar, pulled out his hat, and drank again—several sweet, luscious mouthfuls. They slid down his throat for long seconds, until he had to stop, gulp, and finish. Then, he swallowed again, considered a moment, and pulled his bandana loose. He tied it into place, feeling the damp water against the back of his neck, and smiled.

As he had hoped, the heat from the sun had beaten down so feverishly that it hadn't taken long for small droplets of condensation to form along the bandana. Because of the rock in the middle, the water had been forced to travel down the length of the fabric and collect in the middle. As the minutes rolled on, the blazing sun had turned the salt water fresh, and it had filtered through the bandana, and fallen, drop by drop into his hat. He'd never had the chance before—thank goodness—to turn this trick himself, but he'd heard Hezekiah Hopkins brag all about it when his Army regiment was stranded for four days in the woods. Dead-Eye Dan had remembered enough of the trick to put it into practice. Just enough of it. And thank goodness for Sal Brinkman leaving him his hat. Now, he might stand some chance of getting out of this godforsaken place.

He looked up again. Blessedly, the sun was moving into the west, away from the overhead position where it had lurked nearly all of his time on the shore of the salt lake. Dead-Eye Dan narrowed his eyes and tried to remember the plan of the dastardly Laramie Seven. After they had nabbed the cattle, then what? He could feel his brain creaking back into working order. It was a good feeling.

Then, he remembered. If Sal Brinkman had completed his raid on those cattle, there was only one place he would be headed to offload them—the auction in Salt Lake City. And, by a stroke of luck, Dead-Eye Dan found himself on the eastern side of the salt lake. He might still have a chance to reach the city before sundown. But without Whirlwind, it would be slow going.

There was no time to lose. Dead-Eye Dan had a herd of stolen cattle to save. And a ring of rustlers to bring down.

So off he went, into the heat of the salty wilderness alone.

Except for his hat.

Four hours later—he knew, again, because of his crack ability to gauge the time from the position of the sun—a man staggered down the main street of Salt Lake City. Grime caked his boots, a layer of dust spread along his face and neck, and those who passed him could smell the pungent odor of salt.

Yes, Dead-Eye Dan Crowley wasn't anything to look at—or smell, for that matter—but he was a much different man from the parched soul lost on the shore of the salt lake. Once he'd left the salt plains behind, there had been plenty of fresh water to drink, and he'd even found some berries and a few wild potatoes to eat. His hobo-haggard appearance might just work to his advantage here in the big city. U.S. Marshall Dan Crowley might not be well known here, but a man as square-jawed and broad-shouldered as Dead-Eye Dan was sure to draw some raised eyebrows. And with so much on the line, he had to remain inconspicuous.

As the daylight drifted away, Dead-Eye Dan wandered the maze of streets, each turn made by instinct, following in equal measures both his gut and the contingency plan he had worked out with Deputy Charlie Jasperson should things go awry.

And things had gone awry.

Which was why Dead-Eye Dan found himself standing alone in a narrow alley that ran behind the rear entrance to a neat shop. He approached the door, careful to duck under a clothes line strung across the alley at eye level. He knocked three times, then waited, alert for any trace of movement.

The door swung open. Dead-Eye Dan's eyes narrowed. A slim, bookish man stood before him, a wisp of white hair floating from a nearly-bald head, gold-framed glasses peering up at him. The man squinted at him, but said nothing. He was waiting. And Dead-Eye Dan didn't keep him waiting long.

"I like tacos," Dead-Eye Dan said. "But sometimes, they don't agree with my stomach."

The man blinked once. "You shouldn't put so much salsa on them, then."

The two men stared at one another, both unblinking for long seconds. Finally, Dead-Eye Dan smiled. "That's mighty fine, Alphonso. You remembered the code phrase."

" 'Course I did,"

"So where's Charlie?"

"You can't stay here," Rourke said, eyes shifting nervously from Dead-Eye Dan to the alley, then back. "They've been here already—Brinkman and his men. Said if I saw anything out of the ordinary, to let them know. Or they'd be back." He paused, licking his lips. "And I don't want 'em to come back, Dan. *I don't.*"

Dead-Eye Dan leaned down, his rugged jaw inches from the sallow face of Alphonso Rourke, the finest watchmaker in Salt Lake City, and keeper of a hidden Marshall's safe house. True, he had the steadiest hands in the city, but right now, he was anything but calm. Dead-Eye Dan's eyes narrowed. "You listen good, Rourke. I'm not going to let anything happen to you. You got that straight? Dead-Eye Dan stands—.

"For justice, I know that," Rourke said, his face relaxing slightly. "Just the same, you better get out of here. If you're look-ing for Brinkman, he's over at Callahan's. I overheard him say he's got a pile of cattle ready to off-load. You might be too late, but it's worth a shot."

At this, a slow smile spread across Dead-Eye Dan's face. "You bet it's worth a shot. Maybe a few shots, if it comes to that." He touched the tip of his battered brown hat, the brim stained white around the edges. "Much obliged, Alphonso. One other thing—you got a firearm I could borrow?"

Rourke's eyes widened, and he scurried out of sight. He returned moments later toting a brown Winchester rifle and a length of rope. He handed them over. "Thought you might need this, too. You think the gun will do?"

"Well, it isn't Alejandro, but I can find my way around." Dead-Eye Dan swung the rifle to his side and clasped the watchmaker's hand. "Your country thanks you, Alphonso."

"Be careful," Rourke said.

"They're the ones who need to be careful," Dead-Eye Dan said with a smile. Then, like a whisper, he vanished into the dusk.

Seventeen minutes later, a shadow flitted out of the darkness that enveloped the offices of Jamie Callahan, next door to his cattle auction house. Inside, Jamie Callahan, fabulously wealthy—and notoriously corrupt—cattle auctioneer stood before his large oak desk, staring eye-to-eye with Sal Brinkman, pretending he didn't know that the Lizard of Laramie was offering him a herd of 75 rustled Hereford beef cattle for sale. Callahan was good at not asking questions and pretending he valued honest dealings. In reality, he was as crooked as a corkscrew. Behind him, his wall was lined with hunting trophies: a bear head, two bucks, and directly behind his desk, a massive moose head mounted to a thick oak board.

The shadow flitted in front of the window, peering inside at the crooked deal in progress. It nodded and smiled grimly, glancing down at the Winchester rifle by its side.

"I believe that wraps it up, Jamie," Sal Brinkman said. "You don't need me to sign anything, do you?"

Callahan laughed. "Why start now? But ... if you wanted to have a seat there in that chair and slip your hand into the pocket of that fine coat I've laid out, you might find yourself getting mighty relaxed right about now."

Brinkman reached inside the pocket, felt the thick wad of bills inside, and smiled broadly. "That's mighty fine, Jamie."

"And the cattle?"

The shadow at the window leaned closer, careful not to miss a word.

"They'll be up at the stockyards, pens twenty-two and twenty-three. My men will be there all night tonight."

Pens twenty-two and twenty-three. The shadow nodded, its lips moving slightly.

"Right then. I believe our business here is finished, so—"

Jamie Callahan's words were cut short by a booted foot kicking open the door. Helpless against the right foot of Dead-Eye Dan Crowley, the door shuddered, then fell off its hinges. U.S. Marshall Dan Crowley stood wrapped in darkness, a Winchester rifle leveled at the crooked duo in the room.

"Hands in the air, Brinkman. You too, Callahan. If you know what's good for you, you won't even think about considering the possibility of movement. Freeze!"

The dastardly duo froze. Dead-Eye Dan moved closer,

pulling a thick coil of rope from his back pocket. But as Crowley's eyes flitted down toward the rope, Sal Brinkman's hand dropped to his gun belt, yanked loose his Colt revolver, and brandished it.

But Dead-Eye Dan didn't need to look at him to know what was happening. Still looking down at the rope clutched in his left hand, he raised his rifle and squeezed off a blast that clipped the pistol out of Sal Brinkman's hand. It flew through the air and hit the wall behind him.

Brinkman staggered backward. "You ... weren't even looking at me," he said. "How—"

"I tried to tell you," Dead-Eye Dan said, "you may have tangled with cougars before, but you've never gone up against the likes of me." With that, he tossed the rope at Brinkman. "Tie yourselves together. Now."

But Jamie Callahan hadn't seen enough yet. Dropping to one knee, he slid his own gleaming Colt pistol from its holster and fired. The shot plucked the hat directly off Dead-Eye Dan's head. He fell hard, rolling to his side and throwing himself against the wall. He scrambled behind a table, a blur of movement letting him know Brinkman was attempting to find the door. Dead-Eye Dan squeezed off a second rifle blast, heard a yelp, and saw Brinkman drop to the ground. Steam rose from a neat hole just beyond his big toe. The man's eyes were as wide as a silver dollar as he stared at his holey boot.

Dead-Eye Dan inched along the wall, waiting for Callahan to return to view. Then, he saw him behind his desk, eyes darting left and right. Dead-Eye Dan poked the rifle up, found his angle, and fired.

A metal ping. A weighty thud. A second yelp, this one a howl of pain. Then, another thud, and finally, silence. Dead-Eye Dan stood.

Jamie Callahan lay slumped across his desk, arms splayed in front of him, body rising and falling with long, slow breaths. Atop him lay a moose head, still attached to its board, covering most of Callahan's prone torso.

Dead-Eye Dan's boots clicked on the wood floor as he ambled toward the two men.

"You've got to watch those moose," he said. "Nasty critters. Get too close and they'll take you down as soon as look at you." He smirked as Callahan groaned up at him. "I've got a date with seventy-five Hereford cattle at pen twenty-two. And you've got a date with the judge, Brinkman," he said. "So let's make this snappy."

Three men strode away from Callahan's Auction House that October night. Two were handcuffed, bound, and headed for justice.

And the third was Dead-Eye Dan Crowley, the face of justice in the lawless West.

Has Dead-Eye Dan put Sal Brinkman behind bars for the final time? Or will the Lizard of Laramie slither out from under his rock for more misdeeds? Enthusiastic readers will thrill to the next adventure featuring Dead-Eye Dan— "Dead-Eye Dan Spends a Night in Coyote Canyon," available next month wherever fine reading materials are sold.

 GLENN MCCARTY was raised in the shadow of Walt Disney World, and has never really grown up. He lives with his wife and children in a small town in Western New York that's pretty much Mayberry. But without Don Knotts. Bummer. He also has a dog who likes to bark at visitors, then boldly run and hide from them. He is the author of *The Misadventured Summer of Tumbleweed Thompson*, and finds campfires and banjo music two of life's simple pleasures. And pie.

 JOE SUTPHIN'S illustrated books for children include *Word of Mouse* by James Patterson, *Monster's Trucks* by Rebecca Van Slyke, *Raffie On The Run* by Jacqueline Resnick and *The Misadventured Summer of Tumbleweed Thompson* by your very own Glenn McCarty. When he is not drawing and writing stories, Joe might be found looking under rocks for interesting critters. He and his wife live in barn in Ohio with a whole bunch of cats.

SEE WHERE IT
ALL BEGAN!

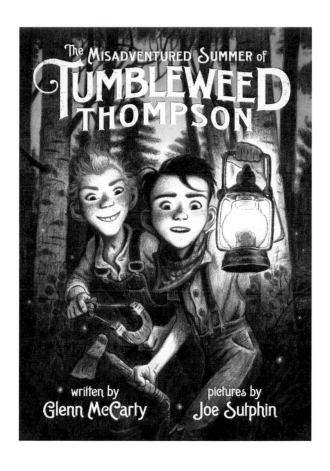

Keep up with all the latest from Glenn McCarty!

www.glennmccarty.com/newsletter